THE WORST!

The softball team gathered around Mr. Davis. His face was red, and he looked very upset.

"That was terrible!" he yelled. "I thought you were supposed to be such a good team! And you were leading! What happened out there?"

"It was those stupid girls," Charlie said angrily. "We could have won that game easily."

"Well, that's the way girls play," Mr. Davis replied. "The real question is, why are they on the team?"

"Yeah!" yelled one of the boys, and then all of them were nodding.

Elizabeth and Jessica looked at each other, aghast. Had they already forgotten that the girls were their most valuable players?

"We've got one entire week to practice for the final game," said Mr. Davis. "But there's only one way we can win."

He paused and glanced meaningfully at the boys.

"We're taking all the girls off the team."

Bantam Books in the Sweet Valley Twins series
Ask your bookseller for the books you have missed

SWEET VALLEY TWINS SUPER CHILLERS

SWEET VALLEY TWINS SUPER EDITIONS

SWEET VALLEY TWINS

Boys Against Girls

Written by
Jamie Suzanne

Created by
FRANCINE PASCAL

A BANTAM BOOK®
TORONTO · NEW YORK · LONDON · SYDNEY · AUCKLAND

RL 4, 008–012

BOYS AGAINST GIRLS

A Bantam Book/September 1988
Reprinted 1991

Sweet Valley High® and Sweet Valley Twins are
trademarks of Francine Pascal.

Conceived by Francine Pascal.

Produced by Daniel Weiss Associates, Inc.
27 West 20th St.
New York, NY 10011

Cover art by James Mathewuse.

ISBN 0-553-15571-7

Published simultaneously in the United States and Canada

Bantam Books are published by Bantam Books, a division of Bantam
Doubleday Dell Publishing Group, Inc. Its trademark, consisting of
the words "Bantam Books" and the portrayal of a rooster, is Regis-
tered in U.S. Patent and Trademark Office and in other countries.
Marca Registrada. Bantam Books, Inc., 666 Fifth Avenue, New York,
New York 10103.

Printed and bound in Great Britain by
Cox & Wyman Ltd., Reading

To Kasey Anne Blaustein

One

◇

The Wakefield family was gathered around the table in their spacious Spanish-style kitchen eating breakfast on a sunny Monday morning.

"We're getting our new homeroom teacher today," Jessica announced to the others as she dug a spoon into her grapefruit.

"That's great," her father said, helping himself to some scrambled eggs. "I'm a little tired of hearing you two girls complain about your substitute teachers."

Elizabeth, Jessica's twin, smiled apologetically. "I guess we did complain a lot. But you know what? It wasn't really the substitutes who were so bad. It was the boys in our class. Whenever there's a sub, they start fooling around."

Steven Wakefield, the twins' older brother, took a break from his breakfast long enough to respond to her comment. "Hah! And I'm sure you're both perfect little ladies when your teacher is away." He turned his attention back to his plate and continued wolfing down his bacon and eggs.

Jessica sniffed. "*We* know how to behave in class," she said primly.

"I'm glad to hear that," Mrs. Wakefield said, her eyes twinkling. "And now you'll be getting a new, permanent teacher for the term. Have you seen her yet?"

"It's not a 'her,'" Jessica said. "It's a 'him'! I was in the principal's office on Friday, and I heard the secretary say that our new homeroom teacher is named Mr. Davis."

Elizabeth looked thoughtful. "Maybe he can keep those boys from acting so goofy."

Steven grinned wickedly. "You never know. He might let the boys get away with murder. After all, he's one of them."

Elizabeth sighed. "Don't be silly. He's a teacher."

Jessica put her elbows on the table, cupped her chin in her hands, and gazed dreamily into space. "Maybe he'll be young and handsome."

Elizabeth rolled her eyes at her sister's comment. "I just hope he's as good a teacher as Ms. Pauley was."

It was just like Jessica to hope their new teacher was good-looking. For the zillionth time, Elizabeth wondered how two sisters could look exactly alike and act so totally different.

Elizabeth and Jessica were mirror images, right down to the dimples in their left cheeks. They had the same sun-streaked blond hair, blue-green eyes, and peaches-and-cream complexion. But the similarities ended there.

Elizabeth was thoughtful and serious. She enjoyed spending time with her friends, but she also liked being alone, whether it was to read or write, or just to think. Jessica, on the other hand, despised being alone. She was always running around, getting involved in schemes, and giggling with her friends about boys, clothes, and makeup.

Just this year they had stopped dressing alike, too. Jessica now wore her hair down in soft waves around her face, and she had recently started to wear a little makeup. Today, she was wearing a short purple skirt with a hot-pink T-shirt. She was a member of the Unicorn Club, and all members had to wear at least one article of purple clothing every day. Privately, Elizabeth thought the Unicorns were snobs, but she tried not to say too many bad things about them.

Elizabeth didn't wear any makeup at all, and she wore her hair pulled back on the sides and fastened with barrettes. As for clothes, she was perfectly content with her neatly pressed jeans and a tailored blouse.

But despite their different personalities, different interests, and different friends, they were still closer to each other than they were to anyone else. Even when they didn't understand each other's motives, they were still the best of friends.

"I hope Mr. Davis likes softball," Elizabeth remarked to Jessica as they left the house for school. "'We've got the big game on Friday. Maybe he'll let us practice outside during homeroom.'"

Jessica tossed her head confidently, and her blond waves tumbled around her shoulders. "We'll win, whether we practice or not," she assured Elizabeth.

She was probably right, Elizabeth thought. The sixth grade homerooms had been playing serious softball all term. Each homeroom had its own team—theirs was the Tigers. Right now, the Tigers were in the championship play-offs with the Wildcats, another homeroom. If the Tigers won Friday's game, they'd be the sixth-grade champions. If not, they'd have to play a seventh game.

Elizabeth felt pretty confident the Tigers would win—and Jessica was one of the reasons. Early in the season, the class had discovered that Jessica had a talent for catching balls in the outfield—and she'd prevented the best hitters on the other teams from scoring.

There were lots of fun things coming up in the next couple of weeks—the championships, tomorrow's homeroom outing to the zoo, the Sixth Grade Follies . . .

Thinking about the Follies reminded Elizabeth of something, and she turned to Jessica.

"Did I tell you Nora Mercandy came up with a great idea for our Follies skit? I hope I'll get to be the director."

"Can I be the star?" Jessica asked eagerly.

Elizabeth hesitated. As much as she loved her sister, she knew she wasn't the most reliable person around. "It would be a lot of work, Jess. Memorizing lines, rehearsals every day after school . . ."

Jessica frowned as she considered her sister's words. "I guess you're right. Forget it. I have more important things to do after school. I wouldn't want to miss any of the Unicorn meetings." Then she brightened. "How about putting me in charge of makeup?"

"Perfect! I think this is going to be great fun!" Elizabeth said with enthusiasm, as she thought about how much there was to look forward to.

When they walked into their homeroom, it was obvious that the new teacher hadn't shown up yet. Kids stood everywhere, laughing and talking. A couple of boys were having a paper airplane throwing contest. Two of Jessica's best friends and fellow Unicorns, Lila Fowler and Ellen Riteman, had their mirrors out and were reapplying lip gloss. Ellen kept fussing with her hair, too.

Jessica ran over to join them while Elizabeth made her way to her usual seat, between Nora Mercandy and Amy Sutton. Amy was looking at Lila and Ellen and shaking her head in amusement.

"I can't believe they're putting on all that makeup and fixing their hair for our new teacher," she said to Elizabeth. She pushed her own stringy, limp blond hair out of her eyes.

"I can't believe it, either," Elizabeth agreed, glancing back at them. Now Jessica had her mirror out, too, and she was anxiously patting her hair. "Jessica spent our entire breakfast dreaming about how good-looking the new teacher will be."

"Well, I just hope he's nice," Nora murmured. "Does anyone know what subject he teaches?"

"English, I think," Amy replied.

"Great!" Elizabeth said with enthusiasm. English was her favorite subject—and anyone who taught it couldn't be too bad.

Ronnie Edwards and Tom McKay ambled over. "Want to hear something funny?" Tom asked. "Jim Sturbridge claims he's going to pitch a no-hitter this Friday."

The girls laughed. Jim was the pitcher for the Wildcats, and he was famous for bragging and showing off.

"No way," Amy said spiritedly.

Ronnie grinned at her. "Well, I guess he just forgot that we have Amy Sutton, world-famous hitter, to slam his pitches right out of the park?"

"And my sister, who can catch anything," Elizabeth piped up loyally.

"Hey, what about me?" Tom asked, pretending to look offended.

"Oh, you guys aren't half-bad, either," Amy said, her pale blue eyes twinkling.

"That Sturbridge is in for a big surprise," Ronnie announced. "We're going to slaughter 'em."

"Hey, I think the teacher's coming!" someone called from the door. The entire class scrambled to their seats. In less than a second, the room was silent.

Mr. Clark, the principal, entered the room first. Another man followed close behind him.

Elizabeth looked at the new teacher curiously. He was a tall, distinguished-looking man wearing a neatly pressed gray suit. He walked stiffly to the desk in front of the room, looking very serious.

"Class, I'd like you to meet Mr. Davis, your new homeroom teacher this term. I expect all of you to be on your best behavior, and I hope you'll make him feel welcome." Mr. Clark turned to the new teacher. "They're all yours," he said with a smile before walking briskly out of the room.

The students stared at Mr. Davis. Mr. Davis stared right back.

"Good morning, class," Mr. Davis said, still looking terribly serious. "After I've called the roll, I'd like to tell you about my plans for this homeroom. I can see already we have some changes to make."

Twenty sets of eyebrows went up.

"What's he talking about?" Amy whispered to Elizabeth. "What kind of changes?"

Elizabeth was puzzled, too. But she just sat quietly, watched, and waited.

Two

◇

"As I call the roll," Mr. Davis continued, "I shall indicate where I want you to sit from now on."

Elizabeth and Amy looked at each other in alarm. He was changing the seating arrangement! Would they be separated?

Slowly, the new teacher started down the list of names, rearranging the class seating as he went.

"This is weird," Amy muttered, and Elizabeth had to agree. Usually, teachers only made kids change seats if they were behaving badly, or whispering all the time. But Mr. Davis wanted to rearrange all of them—and no one in the class had said a word yet!

Elizabeth noticed something else peculiar, too. When Mr. Davis called the boys' names, he'd ask if they had a nickname they preferred. But when he called the girls' names, he didn't bother to ask about nicknames; in fact, he barely looked at them.

Elizabeth moved to the seat Mr. Davis indicated, on the other side of the room. She was pleased to see that she was still right next to Amy, although Nora was now two seats behind her. But as she looked around the room to see who was where, her eyes widened. Mr. Davis's new arrangement had all the boys on one side and all the girls on the other!

Amy noticed this, too. "Why do you think he did that?" she asked Elizabeth in a whisper.

Elizabeth wasn't sure. "I guess he doesn't think boys and girls should sit together. Maybe he's afraid we'd flirt or something." It didn't make sense to her, though. Most of the sixth graders she knew—with the exception of Jessica—just weren't into flirting yet.

Mr. Davis surveyed the room with satisfaction when the roll call was finished. "Now," he said, "I will assign regular homeroom duties." Everyone sat up straighter, hoping to get picked for the good jobs, like carrying messages.

"I see that you have a lot of plants here on the windowsill," Mr. Davis noted. "I suppose you girls brought them in. They should be watered daily."

Ricky Capaldo raised his hand slightly and spoke in a voice barely above a whisper. "I usually water them because I get to school early." For Ricky, that was a major speech. The small, thin boy was one of the shyest of the sixth graders.

Mr. Davis smiled at him kindly. "Well, I think

one of the girls should handle it. I'll give that job to . . ." He paused and looked at the roll. "Ellen Riteman."

Elizabeth glanced at Ellen, who made it obvious that she wasn't pleased with this job.

"And you've got gerbils," Mr. Davis continued, still looking at the roll. "Feeding the gerbils will be Jessica Wakefield's responsibility."

Elizabeth suppressed a grin. She didn't have to turn around and look at Jessica—she could imagine the horror on her twin's face. Jessica hated the gerbils, and she avoided them like the plague. She thought they were dirty and nasty.

"I will need a permanent messenger to take occasional notes to the office," Mr. Davis announced.

That was the job everyone wanted. All over the room hands shot up. Mr. Davis didn't even glance at the girls' side. He immediately selected Charlie Cashman.

"Is he crazy?" Amy asked Elizabeth in a whisper. "If he lets Charlie out of the room, he'll never come back!"

"I guess he just doesn't know about Charlie," Elizabeth whispered back. But it seemed to her that one look at Charlie's mischievous expression would alert any teacher that Charlie Cashman was definitely not the most responsible person in the class.

Other kids looked on in surprise, too. But

Charlie just folded his arms and leaned back with an expression of extreme satisfaction on his face.

"Finally," Mr. Davis continued, after having assigned most of the chores, "we'll need some girls to straighten up the room every day." For what seemed like the first time that day, he looked at the girls' side of the room. When he didn't see any volunteers, he frowned. "Everyone has to play his part," he muttered, and examined his roll list. "Amy Sutton, Elizabeth Wakefield, Nora Mercandy, and Lila Fowler."

Elizabeth heard an outraged gasp. It had to have come from Lila, and Elizabeth knew she must be furious. Lila never had to straighten up anything—not even her own room at home. Her father was one of the richest men in Sweet Valley, and she had at least two live-in housekeepers to pick up after her all the time.

Elizabeth couldn't resist turning around and taking a peek at her. Lila was waving her hand frantically in the air, but Mr. Davis just went on talking.

"You girls will be responsible for making sure we leave this room in the same condition that we found it. Of course, if you need to move anything, like desks, you should ask the boys to help you. I'm sure they'll be happy to oblige."

"Fat chance," Amy muttered, and Elizabeth silently agreed.

Mr. Davis went to his desk and sat down.

"Now that we've taken care of all that, I'd like someone to fill me in on what's going on here at school." It sounded as if he were speaking to the whole class, but he was only looking at the boys' side. He called on Ronnie.

"We're in the middle of the softball play-offs," Ronnie said. "The Tigers—that's us—are playing the Wildcats, another homeroom, on Friday. If we win, we'll be sixth-grade champions."

"Excellent!" Mr. Davis exclaimed, smiling broadly. "You boys must be terrific ballplayers."

"'You boys'!" Amy gasped. "What about us girls?"

Elizabeth cringed, waiting for Mr. Davis to scold Amy for speaking without raising her hand. But Mr. Davis didn't even look at her.

"And the Sixth Grade Follies are next week," Ronnie continued. "We're supposed to come up with a skit."

"Ah, a theatrical production," Mr. Davis said. "Very interesting. What else?"

Ronnie thought for a minute. "Oh, I almost forgot! Tomorrow we've got our homeroom outing to the San Diego Zoo. Elizabeth organized it."

Mr. Davis looked blank. "Who?"

"Elizabeth Wakefield."

Tentatively, Elizabeth raised her hand to identify herself. Mr. Davis looked at her and nodded. Elizabeth took that to mean she was allowed to speak.

"We're supposed to meet here at nine o'clock," she reported. "There will be a bus waiting to take us to the zoo. We collected money last week for admission and lunches. I think the teacher put it in your top drawer, the one with the lock on it."

Mr. Davis reached in his coat pocket and took out a key. Then he opened the drawer and extracted an envelope.

"How much is the admission?" he asked, looking in the envelope.

"Two dollars a person," Elizabeth told him.

Mr. Davis counted out some bills and put them in a separate envelope. Then he got up, went to Elizabeth's desk, and handed her the rest. "You girls buy whatever you need and make sandwiches for lunch." Then he returned to his desk.

Clutching the envelope, Elizabeth was stunned. She couldn't believe what she had just heard. Sandwiches? Why should the girls make sandwiches? The money was collected so they could buy lunches at the zoo!

But she couldn't bring herself to say anything. So she just sat there, looking glumly at the money.

"Let's discuss this zoo trip," Mr. Davis said. "That's a big zoo we're going to, and we won't be able to see everything there. We'd better get organized and decide now which areas we're going to visit. Any suggestions?"

Three girls and one boy raised their hands. Elizabeth wasn't surprised when Mr. Davis called on the boy.

"How about the tigers?"

"Fine," Mr. Davis said, writing that down. "What else?"

"The apes," Charlie Cashman yelled, without even raising his hand. Mr. Davis nodded, and noted that.

"I want to see the pandas," a girl in the back called out, but Mr. Davis had already called on another boy. He continued to call on the boys as if the girls didn't even exist.

"This is crazy!" Elizabeth whispered to Amy. "The boys are getting to decide everything!"

Amy nodded angrily. She was waving her hand frantically and finally resorted to calling out, "Mr. Davis! Mr. Davis!"

Mr. Davis turned to her with a look of annoyance. "Don't you know you're not supposed to speak without raising your hand?"

Amy's pale face went pink. "I *did* raise my hand! I wanted to ask if we could see the giraffes."

Mr. Davis looked at his list and shook his head. "I'm afraid there won't be time to see any more than what we already have listed."

Suddenly, a girl sitting behind Elizabeth shrieked, "Yuk! Look at the spider!"

Elizabeth saw it, too. It was a pretty big spider, and it was crawling up the wall just a few feet from her. So she grabbed a piece of paper from her desk and got up to get it.

"What do you think you're doing?" Mr. Davis asked sharply.

Elizabeth looked at him in confusion. "I was just going to get rid of the spider."

"Well, sit down," Mr. Davis barked and turned to the boys. "Uh, Tom, would you go and get that spider?"

Thank goodness the bell rang just then. Elizabeth didn't think she could spend one more minute in that classroom. But Mr. Davis still had one thing left to say.

"I need some boys to help me carry books to another room." He pointed to Ronnie and Ricky Capaldo.

"I could carry twice as many books as that skinny little Ricky Capaldo," Amy muttered as she got up from her seat. "Why doesn't he ever call on girls?"

"I don't get it," Nora said, joining them. "How come he gave all the good jobs to the boys?"

Jessica, Lila, and Ellen, all looking furious, came over to them. "This is outrageous," Lila said through gritted teeth. "Why should *I* have to straighten up this room?"

Elizabeth wasn't thrilled with that job, either, but she was even more upset about the way Mr. Davis was treating *all* the girls. "How come it's the *girls* who have to do the cleaning up?"

"And feed the gerbils!" Jessica wailed. "How disgusting!"

"I had my hand up, and he wouldn't even call on me," Ellen said.

"I'm going to make an official complaint," Lila stated firmly.

"To whom?" Jessica asked.

Lila tossed her head. "Well, my father, first of all."

Amy made a face. "It's so babyish to complain about a teacher to your parents."

Remembering what her father had said just that morning, Elizabeth knew she'd better not start complaining about Mr. Davis at home.

"Do you have any better ideas?" Lila snapped.

"No," Amy admitted and turned to Elizabeth. "Do you?"

Elizabeth shook her head sadly. "No." She realized she was clutching the money envelope so tightly, her knuckles had turned white. Suddenly she remembered the other job Mr. Davis had given her.

"Hey," she said weakly, "who's going to help me make sandwiches?"

Three

◇

Elizabeth pulled a slice of bread from the bag and quickly spread mustard on it. She handed it to Amy, who layered bologna and cheese on it. Then Amy passed it to Nora, who added another slice of bread and cut the sandwich in half.

Elizabeth glanced at the kitchen clock. "We'll have to hurry if we're going to be at school by nine."

"It's too bad we couldn't make these last night," Amy grumbled. "Then we wouldn't have to rush."

Elizabeth shook her head. "If we'd made them last night, they'd be soggy by today."

"So what?" Amy said. "The boys *deserve* soggy sandwiches. I can't believe Mr. Davis is making us do this."

"I wish we had more help," Nora commented. "We still have to bag them and add the other stuff."

A few seconds later, Jessica appeared, wearing a light blue jumpsuit.

"Jessica, put a sandwich in each of the brown bags with an apple, a brownie, and a bag of chips," Elizabeth instructed her.

Jessica groaned, but she joined the production line. "What kind of sandwiches are these?"

"Some are bologna and cheese," Nora told her, "and some are peanut butter and jelly."

Jessica giggled. "Why don't you just mix them all together?"

Amy rolled her eyes. "That's disgusting, Jessica."

"It would serve those dumb boys right," Jessica said.

Elizabeth tried to be fair. "I guess we shouldn't blame the boys. It's not their fault Mr. Davis favors them."

"She's right," Nora said. "The only person to blame is Mr. Davis himself."

Jessica's eyes glinted with a familiar mischievous twinkle. "Then let's make Mr. Davis a special sandwich."

Elizabeth eyed her sister suspiciously. "Jessica, just what do you have in mind?"

But Jessica had already gone to work. She took a piece of bread and spread it with peanut butter and jelly, then she added slices of bologna and cheese. Then she went to the refrigerator and extracted a jar of pickles.

"Jessica!" Amy squealed. "That's awful!" But she was grinning as Jessica pulled out a pickle, neatly sliced it, and added it to the mess on the sandwich.

Nora was watching in awe. "That's the most revolting thing I've ever seen."

Elizabeth gasped. "Jess, you're not really going to give that to Mr. Davis, are you?"

Jessica stepped back and examined her work critically. "Just one more thing." She went back to the refrigerator and pulled out a bag of flaked coconut left over from a cake Mrs. Wakefield had baked.

In unison, Amy and Nora shrieked, "Jessica! Yuk!" And then they started laughing hysterically as Jessica sprinkled the coconut on the sandwich. She carefully wrapped the sandwich and placed it in a brown paper bag. "Perfection!" she announced, holding up the bag.

At first, Elizabeth watched in horror. Then as she imagined Mr. Davis biting into the sandwich, she just had to burst out laughing.

"We can't do this, we can't do this," she kept saying, but she was laughing so hard tears were streaming down her face.

"Mark the bag so we'll know it's his," Amy suggested, still giggling. Jessica took a pen and made an X on the bag.

"What's so funny?" Mrs. Wakefield was standing in the doorway, watching them with interest.

The girls immediately choked back their giggles. "Oh, we're just being silly," Jessica said, winking at the others behind her mother's back.

"It looks like you girls are going to need a ride to school," Mrs. Wakefield said, noticing the growing mound of bags. "Let me know when you're ready, and I'll drive you."

As soon as she was out of hearing distance, Elizabeth turned to Jessica. "You're terrible, Jess! What if Mom had seen us?"

"Oh, Lizzie, come on. Don't be such a goody two-shoes. It'll be funny."

"Oh, I guess you're right," Elizabeth murmured, still not completely convinced.

"Did you tell your parents about Mr. Davis?" Amy asked her.

"No," Elizabeth replied. "My father said he didn't want to hear any more complaints about teachers."

Nora scraped the last of the jelly out of a jar and slapped it on the bread. "Well, I don't care if Mr. Davis is a teacher. I think he's a creep."

"Who's a creep?" asked Steven, sauntering in and reaching for a bag of chips. Jessica managed to snatch it away before he could get his hands on it.

Elizabeth figured it was safe to complain about their teacher to Steven. After all, he was always complaining about his teachers. "Our new homeroom teacher, Mr. Davis. He actually separated the boys from the girls in class."

"Yeah. And the boys get to do all the good stuff," Amy added. "And we're stuck making lunches."

Steven nodded in approval. "Sounds to me like Mr. Davis has the right idea."

The girls groaned and made faces at him, but Steven just eyed the sandwiches appreciatively. "Hey, can I have one of those?"

Elizabeth looked at the others and tried to suppress a giggle. "Why don't you ask Jessica to make you one of her extra-special ones?"

It was lucky for Steven that he was satisfied with the bologna and cheese he grabbed from the table.

When the girls finished packing the lunches, they piled the small brown bags into two big shopping bags. Then they piled both of the bags and themselves into the car where Mrs. Wakefield was waiting.

"It was certainly nice of you girls to volunteer to make the lunches," Mrs. Wakefield commented as she drove them to school.

"We didn't—" Jessica started to say, but Elizabeth poked her in the ribs. "We didn't have much trouble," Jessica finished lamely.

Their classmates were waiting in front of the school with Mr. Davis, who was taking roll before they boarded the bus. He told the girls to get in first and fill up the back seats.

"Naturally, the girls have to sit in the back," Amy muttered as she and Elizabeth boarded.

"Well, at least that way we can talk about him, and he won't hear us," Nora said.

Sure enough, most of the conversation at the back of the bus centered on Mr. Davis. "What's his problem, anyway?" one girl asked.

"I heard he used to teach at an all-boys school before he came to Sweet Valley," another girl said.

"Well, he'd better get used to girls fast," Lila snapped, "or we're going to have to do something drastic."

"We already have," Jessica said, and she told Lila about the special sandwich she'd made for him. The word spread through the back of the bus, and soon all the girls were eyeing Jessica with the utmost respect.

Elizabeth shifted uncomfortably in her seat. She was still feeling a little funny about that sandwich. She didn't see how it could change Mr. Davis's attitude toward girls. But she tried to push her guilty feelings aside. It was a beautiful, sunny day. They were on their way to a fabulous place, and she was determined to enjoy it.

Most of the kids had been to the San Diego Zoo before, but it was the kind of place a person could go to again and again without ever tiring of it.

As the class moved from one area of the zoo to another, Elizabeth noticed that the boys were staying very close to Mr. Davis. And they listened to every word as he pointed out the various animals.

"I think the boys like Mr. Davis," Amy told Elizabeth. "I heard Jerry McAllister tell Charlie Cashman he thought Mr. Davis was really neat."

"You're kidding!" Elizabeth exclaimed. "How can they think he's neat?"

"You know how boys are," Amy replied.

Elizabeth had an awful thought. "Amy, what if the boys start acting like Mr. Davis? You know, treating us as if we're not as good as they are?"

"They'd better not," Amy said. "We might not be able to do anything about Mr. Davis, but our own classmates can't get away with it."

Throughout the morning, as they toured the zoo, Mr. Davis talked about what they were seeing, but it always seemed as if he were just talking to the boys. He wasn't actually nasty to the girls—he was always polite. But he just seemed to act as if they weren't as important as the boys.

When it was lunchtime, Nora and Amy got the shopping bags from the bus and handed out the sandwiches in the picnic area.

"I don't like bologna," Jerry said when he unwrapped his sandwich. "You got anything else?"

"Peanut butter and jelly," Elizabeth told him.

Jerry considered this. "Okay, give me one

of those. It's not my favorite, but it's better than bologna."

Jessica frowned at him. "Maybe you should have made the sandwiches yourself."

Jerry sneered. "That's woman's work."

Elizabeth reached into the sack for another bag. The one she pulled out had the X on it. She hesitated. Did she dare give that nasty sandwich to Mr. Davis? Maybe she should just keep that one for herself and pretend to eat it.

Jessica took the decision out of her hands. She snatched the bag and presented it to Mr. Davis.

"Here's one for you, Mr. Davis," she said sweetly.

"Thank you," Mr. Davis replied. "Here's some money, girls. Why don't you go over to that refreshment stand and buy us all sodas."

It took Elizabeth, Jessica, Amy, and Nora four trips to bring back enough sodas for everyone. By the time they had completed the last trip, they were all furious.

"What does he think we are, slaves?" Amy fumed.

"I can't wait for him to bite into that sandwich," Jessica said. And even Elizabeth had to admit that Mr. Davis didn't deserve anything better.

She sat down at a table and opened her own bag. Looking around she noticed that the boys were seated separately from the girls. She had wanted to talk to Ronnie about the Sixth Grade Follies—but now it was impossible.

She glanced at Mr. Davis, who was unwrapping his sandwich. Quickly, she looked down at her own, not really wanting to see him take that fatal bit. But Amy was sitting right next to her, and in a whisper she described what was happening.

"He put the sandwich down . . . he's opening his chips . . . he's eating a chip . . . now he's finishing his soda . . . he's picking up his sandwich!" She clutched Elizabeth's arm. "He's biting it!"

Elizabeth raised her eyes and looked directly at Mr. Davis. His expression was very peculiar, and she could have sworn his face actually turned a little green. Quickly, he took a napkin and held it to his mouth.

"Probably spitting it out," Amy said gleefully. Both girls watched as he took a long drink of his soda.

Jessica and Lila and some of the other girls were trying desperately to hold back their laughter. Elizabeth's own face was burning.

"That wasn't very nice of us," she whispered sadly.

"It serves him right," Amy stated firmly.

And even Elizabeth had to agree when they finished their lunches and Mr. Davis told the girls to clean up.

"I'm not cleaning up," Lila declared, folding her arms across her chest. "And I'm going to tell my father about this. He'll get him fired."

"No, don't do that," Jessica said. "We should take care of this ourselves."

"How?" Lila asked.

Jessica looked thoughtful. "I'm not sure. But we'll come up with something." Elizabeth gazed at her sister uneasily. What kind of scheme would Jessica cook up now?

That afternoon, they saw bears, zebras, lions, and a few animals Elizabeth couldn't even identify. They walked all over, admiring the sights, gazing in fascination at all the remarkable creatures. Mr. Davis treated them all—even the girls—to ice cream. That made Elizabeth feel a little better. At least the girls weren't being excluded from everything.

"Maybe Mr. Davis isn't so bad, after all," she said to Amy as they got back on the bus. "He just hasn't been around girls that much."

"Maybe," Amy said, but her voice was doubtful.

"He bought us *all* ice cream," Elizabeth reminded her.

"That was nice," Amy admitted, "but he doesn't have to buy us anything. All he has to do is treat us like people."

As the bus moved away from the zoo, Mr.

Davis got up from his front seat and addressed the students.

"Starting tomorrow, we're going to try something new in homeroom," he said. "From now on, we're going to have class discussions during the period. Tomorrow's topic will be poetry."

There were a few groans here and there, but Elizabeth clapped her hands together in delight. She loved poetry!

"I've made copies of two different poems, which I'm going to hand out," Mr. Davis continued. "I want each of you to read your poem carefully and be prepared to read it aloud in homeroom."

He took a stack of papers from his briefcase and walked to the back of the bus. He handed them to Nora. "Would you pass these out among the girls, please." Then he went back to the front of the bus, got another stack of papers, and handed them out to the boys.

Elizabeth turned to Amy. "See? A person who likes poetry can't be all bad."

Amy just shrugged. She didn't look convinced. But Elizabeth sat up straight and happily waited for her poem. Homeroom was definitely looking better.

Four

◇

"I hope Mr. Davis doesn't call on me in class," Jessica said as she and Elizabeth entered school on Wednesday. "I don't want to read that stupid poem out loud."

For once, Elizabeth had to agree with her. It *was* a stupid poem, and she was very disappointed with it. With all the beautiful poems in the world, why did Mr. Davis pick one about fairies dancing in a garden? It was babyish, and Elizabeth, too, hoped she wouldn't have to read it in class.

"You're supposed to feed the gerbils," Elizabeth reminded her sister as they entered homeroom. Jessica made a sour face.

"Ooh, I hate going near those animals," she moaned. "Why did he have to pick me?"

"Well, I'm not too thrilled about cleaning up after class, either," Elizabeth said. As she went to her seat, she noticed that all the boys were hanging out together on their side, while the girls stayed on theirs. She wanted to talk to Tom about

Friday's softball game, but she felt funny about going to the boys' side of the room. She had a feeling she wouldn't be welcome there.

"Did you read that poem?" Amy asked her.

Elizabeth wrinkled her nose. "I thought it was pretty awful."

Amy agreed. "I felt silly reading it to myself."

"I wonder if the boys got such a terrible poem?" Elizabeth wondered out loud. She soon found out. Mr. Davis came in just as the bell was ringing.

"Did you enjoy reading your poems?" Mr. Davis inquired after calling roll.

Nora made a face, and so did some of the other girls, but none of them responded.

But the boys had a different response. Elizabeth was surprised to see several of them nodding enthusiastically.

"Let's hear them out loud," Mr. Davis said, and he called on Ronnie Edwards. Blushing slightly, Ronnie stood up and began to read.

It was a great poem, about a soldier fighting in the American Revolution. It was all about freedom and independence, and the importance of fighting for what you believe in. Ronnie stumbled a little over the words, but it didn't matter. The poem was so strong and powerful, it still sounded thrilling.

"Why couldn't we get a poem like that?" Amy asked Elizabeth in a whisper.

"I don't know," Elizabeth whispered back. "Maybe he's just trying to show us the difference between a good poem and a bad one."

When Ronnie finished, everyone applauded. Elizabeth suspected they were clapping more for the poem than the reader.

Mr. Davis seemed pleased. "Let's discuss this poem. What did it mean to you? How did it make you feel?"

Hands were flying all over the room. As usual, Mr. Davis just called on the boys.

"I liked the battle," Tom said. "I felt like I was actually there, fighting with the guy."

Mr. Davis nodded in approval. "Yes, it was very vividly described. Anyone else have a comment?"

When the boys finished talking about the poem, Mr. Davis turned to the girls' side of the room. "Now let's hear the poem I selected especially for the girls. Can I have a volunteer?"

No one raised a hand. Normally, Elizabeth wouldn't mind reading a poem out loud. But this particular one would be too embarrassing to read in front of the other students. It was just too silly.

Mr. Davis frowned. "Come now, girls, I know you're all shy, but we must have a reader."

We're not shy, Elizabeth thought. *We just know when a poem is so dumb it will make everyone laugh at us.* But she didn't say anything. She just stared at her desk, hoping Mr. Davis wouldn't call on her.

"Amy Sutton, please read your poem," Mr. Davis ordered.

Elizabeth gazed at her friend in sympathy. Amy looked as if she wanted to die.

"'In my garden, every day,'" she began softly, in a voice barely above a whisper.

"Louder, please," Mr. Davis ordered.

Amy paused, gritted her teeth, and began again, reading very rapidly. "'In my garden, every day, the little fairies come and play . . .'"

"Slow down," Mr. Davis said. "And start over."

Now Amy's eyes were flashing. "'In my garden, every day, the little fairies come and play. They romp among the leafy bowers, dancing with my pretty flowers . . .'"

Out of the corner of her eye, Elizabeth could see the boys grinning and smirking. Some didn't even try to smother their laughs. Poor Amy, she thought. When her friend finally finished the poem, she sat down abruptly, her face beet-red.

"Thank you," Mr. Davis said politely. "Now, what can anyone tell us about this poem?"

With the exception of a few snickers from the boys' side, the room was dead silent. Mr. Davis drummed his fingers on his desk impatiently. "Amy, certainly you felt something while you were reading it. Share your feelings with us."

Amy looked as if she were ready to explode. When she finally spoke, she sounded as though she was having a hard time controlling her voice.

"I felt silly," she said. "It's a dumb poem. Why didn't you give us an exciting poem, like the one the boys had?"

Mr. Davis raised his eyebrows. "I felt your poem would be more appropriate for girls. Does anyone else have a comment?"

Amy had pretty much spoken for the entire group. No one had anything to add. Mr. Davis shook his head sadly. "You girls certainly don't have much to say for yourselves. Well, then, let's go on to other business. I understand that we need to prepare for the Sixth Grade Follies, and we should begin by selecting someone to be in charge."

Elizabeth brightened. This was something she'd been looking forward to. Amy raised her hand and began waving it so wildly, Mr. Davis had to notice and call on her.

"Mr. Davis, I nominate Elizabeth to be the director. Everyone knows she can do a great job."

Elizabeth tried to look modest as Nora called out, "I second the nomination."

The teacher's face was stern. "I don't recall saying anything about an election for director. I've already decided to ask Tom McKay to direct the skit."

Elizabeth gasped. Tom McKay? He'd never said anything about wanting to direct the skit. She looked across the room at him.

Tom was staring at Mr. Davis in surprise and confusion. Elizabeth could understand why. Tom was a nice guy, and a friend of hers, but he wasn't much of a leader, and he had a reputation for being disorganized. Mr. Davis probably didn't know that. Elizabeth waited for Tom to tell the teacher that he didn't want the job.

But one of the other boys said, "Yea, Tom," and another boy slapped him on the back. So Tom just grinned a little uneasily and agreed to be the director.

Elizabeth was stunned. Here was her big opportunity to direct again—and Mr. Davis wasn't even going to give her a chance!

Mr. Davis must have seen the disappointment in her face. "I'm sorry, Elizabeth," he said, "but I feel directing needs a strong hand with a lot of male muscle behind it. Perhaps you'd like to be Tom's assistant. You could bring refreshments for the cast, and run errands."

Bring refreshments? Run errands? Elizabeth couldn't believe her ears. Is that all he thought she was good for? Proudly, she raised her head and looked Mr. Davis directly in the eyes. "No, thank you."

Mr. Davis just shrugged. "Let's discuss the skit you'll be doing."

Nora raised her hand. "I've written a skit," she began, but Mr. Davis interrupted her.

"That's nice, but the boys said that they've

already got a skit. Ross, why don't you tell the rest of the class about it."

Ross Bradley stood up and waved a few sheets of paper in the air. "I got this from my brother. He's in college, and his fraternity did this skit. It's really cool. See, a bunch of guys are in this jungle, trying to capture an ape. Only they can't, 'cause the ape's very strong, and he keeps knocking them all down. So all the guys dress up like apes and trick the real ape into following them. My brother says all his friends at college thought it was funny."

Elizabeth didn't think it sounded funny at all. She thought it sounded very stupid. And it didn't have even one part for a girl in it.

But that didn't seem to bother Mr. Davis at all. "Fine, Ross, fine," was all he said.

Elizabeth turned around in her seat and looked at Nora. Nora's mouth was open, and her eyes were shining, as if she were just about to burst into tears. Elizabeth knew exactly how she felt.

"It's almost time for the bell," Mr. Davis said. "You girls better start straightening up." Elizabeth and Amy exchanged frustrated glances.

"Lila, aren't you a member of the clean-up crew, too?" Mr. Davis asked.

Lila looked positively ill, but she got up and followed the other girls as they walked around the room. They picked up a few crumpled pieces of paper from the floor. As Elizabeth passed Jerry McAllister's desk, he casually pushed his pencil so it fell off his desk and hit the floor.

"Hey, Elizabeth, pick up my pencil."

Elizabeth glared at him. "Pick it up yourself," she hissed.

Jerry looked startled at this unusual response from Elizabeth, but he quickly recovered. "It's your job," he said with a smirk. "You're the homeroom maid, aren't you?"

Somehow, Elizabeth managed to control her temper. Down the aisle, she saw another boy toss a wadded-up paper on the floor just as Amy walked by his desk. Amy ignored it.

"You missed this," the boy called to her, grinning. Amy whirled around, picked up the paper, and held her arm back as if she were going to throw it at him. Luckily, the bell rang.

Out in the hallway, Elizabeth, Nora, and Amy huddled together. "My skit's much better than Ross's," Nora said mournfully.

"And I was counting on directing it," Elizabeth added in the same tone. "I just don't understand Mr. Davis at all."

"I do," Amy said unexpectedly. "I mean, I think Mr. Davis is an outright sexist."

Nora's mouth dropped open. "You're nuts! He's not even good-looking!"

Amy rolled her eyes. "Not *sexy*, dummy. *Sexist*. He thinks boys are better than girls. That's why he's letting the boys do all the important things."

Her explanation made sense to Elizabeth— but it didn't make her feel any better. "What are we going to do about it?" she asked.

"I don't know," Amy said. "The worst part is we're going to be stuck with this teacher all year."

"I hate to think about what that Follies skit is going to be like," Nora murmured. "And letting Tom direct it! That's crazy! He doesn't know anything about directing."

"I'm going to talk to Tom," Elizabeth said suddenly. "I don't even think he *wants* to do it."

"Here he comes now," Nora said. Tom was coming out of the homeroom with a couple of other boys. Elizabeth turned to him and smiled brightly. After all, she wasn't mad at Tom. It wasn't his fault that Mr. Davis had picked him.

"Tom," she said, "are you sure you want to direct the skit?"

Tom just shrugged. That was odd, Elizabeth thought. They were pretty good friends.

"Sure," he said, but his tone wasn't very convincing. "Look, Elizabeth, I know you wanted to be in charge. But Mr. Davis is right. Girls can't handle big jobs like that." With that, he turned and walked off with his friends.

Elizabeth stared after him. Then she looked at Amy and Nora and shook her head sadly. "You know what, guys? I have an awful feeling that this sexist business must be catching."

Five

◇

On Thursday afternoon, Elizabeth and Jessica came home from school with a plan. Elizabeth went directly to the kitchen to get sodas and a snack while Jessica went looking for their mother.

She found Mrs. Wakefield in the study, flipping through an interior design magazine.

"Mom, is it OK if we have some friends over this afternoon?" She hoped it was, since she'd already invited them and they were probably on their way at that moment.

Mrs. Wakefield looked up from her magazine. "Of course it's OK, dear. I'm surprised you're even asking. You know you don't need permission to ask a couple of friends over."

Jessica bit her lower lip and gave her mother a lopsided grin. "Well, it's not just a couple of friends, Mom. It's all the girls in our homeroom."

Her mother's eyebrows went up. "*All* of them? What's going on—a project for school?"

"Something like that," Jessica said. Her

mother looked at her curiously, but Jessica didn't offer any more information.

"Well, that's fine," Mrs. Wakefield said finally. "Why don't you girls use the den?"

Jessica flashed her a grateful smile and ran out, yelling, "Thanks, Mom," over her shoulder.

She joined Elizabeth in the kitchen, then helped herself to a potato chip from the bag her sister was emptying into a bowl. "It's OK with Mom," Jessica told her, "and I didn't say what we were planning to do."

"Good," Elizabeth replied, although she felt sort of funny keeping a secret from her mother. But, like Jessica, she knew Mrs. Wakefield wouldn't approve of their idea.

The girls had just finished setting out the chips and pretzels and sodas in the den when the doorbell rang. Lila and Ellen arrived first, followed by Amy and Nora, and then the four other girls in their class trooped in.

Everyone gathered in the den, sitting around and looking at each other awkwardly. Elizabeth realized they'd never all socialized together, outside of homeroom. But they all had one thing in common: a dislike for Mr. Davis; and that was reason enough to meet outside of school.

"He's ruined our homeroom," one of the girls said.

"And it's not just Mr. Davis anymore," Amy said. "Now, all the boys are acting like him."

"They're even more obnoxious than usual," Elizabeth noted. "You know, Tom McKay used to be a good friend. Now, even he acts snotty."

"Charlie and Jim are the worst," Jessica complained. "They keep ordering us around as if we're their personal slaves or something."

"And Mr. Davis lets them get away with it," another girl moaned.

"He even expects us to pick up after them," Lila said. "He thinks that's a 'girl's duty.' Well, I'm getting sick of it."

Elizabeth was on the verge of reminding her that she hadn't once helped straighten up after class, but she decided not to mention it. After all, they were all sick of what was going on, and it was important that they stick together to fight for a change.

"So what are we going to do about this?" Ellen asked.

"First off," Elizabeth said, "I think we should go on strike. No more straightening up, watering plants, or making refreshments."

"And I've got another idea," Jessica said. "We have to teach Mr. Davis and the boys a lesson. I think we should act just the way we're being treated."

Now everyone looked confused. "I don't get it," Nora said. "What do you mean?"

Jessica explained. "Well, they keep telling us we can't do anything important, right? They think girls are dumb and silly and helpless. So, let's start acting that way!"

"That's a crazy idea, Jessica," Amy exclaimed. "Do you think it'll work?"

Jessica shrugged. "It's worth a try, and I think it might be fun, too," she added with a laugh as she turned to face Ellen. "You're supposed to water the plants, right? Well, tomorrow, you could say you can't do it because the watering can is too heavy for you to lift."

"I get it," another girl said excitedly, "and when he tells you to straighten up the room, you say you can't because . . . because . . . because you just polished your nails!"

"Exactly!" Jessica said. "We'll whisper to one another, giggle a lot, and act silly." A brilliant notion struck her. "And watch me during class. Whenever I do this"—she touched her index finger to her right eyebrow—"everyone start giggling! It'll drive the boys crazy!"

Everyone started talking excitedly.

"We should all wear dresses tomorrow," Lila suggested. "The most feminine ones we have."

Amy, a notorious tomboy, groaned at that idea, but she reluctantly agreed. "Elizabeth, do you really think this is going to work?"

"I'm not sure," Elizabeth replied. "But at least maybe it will make him see how stupid his ideas about girls are. We're going to show him how girls would act if they really were helpless."

Just then, they heard Steven's voice in the kitchen. "Hey! What happened to all the sodas?"

"We have them in here," Elizabeth called out to him.

Steven ambled in the door, then stopped when he saw the roomful of girls. "What's going on here—a gigglers' convention?"

Jessica opened her mouth, ready to give him a snappy retort. Then she had a better idea and clamped it shut. She turned to the group, coughed to get their attention, and then touched her right eyebrow. There was an immediate outburst of loud, shrill giggles.

Steven was taken aback by this totally unexpected reaction. When he recovered, he grinned uneasily and moved toward the sodas. Taking one, he started to back out of the room, but he stopped when Jessica called out to him.

"Steven, would you open this soda for me? I just can't do it by myself."

Steven stared at her. "What are you talking about? You open sodas all the time."

Jessica's voice dripped with honey. "I guess I'm just too weak. You're so big and strong and powerful. Oh, please open it for me, pretty please?" She held the soda out to him and batted her eyelashes furiously.

Steven's eyes darted back and forth between her and Elizabeth. "OK, what's the joke? Did you shake it up so it's going to spray me when I open it?"

Jessica's eyes were wide with innocence. "Steven, how could you say that? I could never think of doing something like that. I'm not clever enough."

Steven's expression was suspicious, but he took the can and opened it. "Oh, Steven," Jessica sighed, "you're wonderful." She touched her eyebrow again, and the rest of the girls responded with giggles.

Steven looked as though he'd been trapped in a cage with wild hyenas. Nervously, he backed out of the room.

As soon as he was out of earshot, Jessica turned to the others triumphantly. "See? It's going to drive them *nuts!*"

The next morning, in homeroom, Elizabeth surveyed the girls' side with satisfaction. They were all wearing their most frilly dresses. The bell hadn't rung yet, but Mr. Davis was at his desk, and most of the boys were in their seats. It was time to go to work.

Jessica got up and pranced to Mr. Davis's desk. In a voice loud enough for everyone to hear, she said, "Mr. Davis, I can't feed the gerbils anymore."

Mr. Davis looked up, puzzled. "Why not?"

"I'm *scared* of little animals," Jessica squealed. "They might *bite* me. Maybe one of the boys could feed them instead. They're braver than girls." She turned slightly so the girls could see her, and put her finger to her eyebrow. The whole side of the room erupted in giggles.

"I suppose that could be arranged, if you're really frightened," Mr. Davis said. "Ross, would you feed the gerbils?"

Ross glanced curiously at Jessica, and then went to the gerbils. Meanwhile, Ellen skipped over to the windowsill where the watering can stood. She made a big show of trying to lift it.

"Mr. Davis," she wailed, "I can't water the plants. This can is too heavy to pick up. I guess one of the boys should do it. They're so much stronger than we are."

Again, Jessica gave the signal, and the girls giggled.

"Yes, yes," Mr. Davis said impatiently. "Uh, Larry, water the plants, please."

The bell rang, and the boys' side of the room settled down. Not the girls' side, though. They immediately leaned toward their neighbor or twisted around, and started whispering.

Elizabeth peeked at Mr. Davis, who was trying to get their attention for the roll call. He was looking at them, shaking his head, as if this behavior was exactly what he expected from girls. But the boys were all staring at the girls with puzzled expressions.

"Girls, girls, I must have your attention," Mr. Davis called out. On cue, the girls giggled again. He sighed, then began calling roll. As each girl's name was called, she said "here" in a high squeaky voice, punctuated with another giggle. To Elizabeth's surprise, Mr. Davis didn't get angry, or even annoyed. He smiled sweetly, shook his head again, and murmured, "Well, girls will be girls."

But the boys knew something was up. Every time Elizabeth sneaked a peek at their side, she caught one or two eyeing them warily.

"I have an announcement to make," Mr. Davis said when he finished the roll. "We're going to have a visitor on Monday. Mr. Clark will be observing this class. I've told him how we're using our homeroom time more productively now, and he wants to see it for himself. We need an especially good topic for Monday's discussion. Any suggestions?"

While the boys thought about this, half the girls raised their hands eagerly. And they didn't wait to be called on.

"Mr. Davis," Jessica said, "could we talk about fashion? On television, they said the skirts are going to be shorter this spring. I think we need to discuss that."

Mr. Davis smiled in amusement. "I know that's a subject of great interest to you girls, but—"

Amy didn't let him finish. "I can think of something much more important," she called out. "Makeup!"

Mr. Davis put his hand to his mouth and coughed, as if he were trying to conceal a chuckle. "Makeup?"

"Yes!" Amy exclaimed, her voice quivering with excitement. "Like, what's better, pink blusher or peach? And should we wear blue or green eyeshadow? I've been worrying about that all week!"

The boys were watching Amy with their mouths open, and Elizabeth knew why. Of all the girls in the homeroom, Amy would be the last one to care about makeup.

Mr. Davis didn't look disturbed by this at all. "I don't think girl talk is really appropriate for a homeroom discussion," he said kindly. "But may I add that you girls look very pretty today. Now, boys, can you think of a good topic?"

Tom raised his hand. "How about democracy?"

Mr. Davis looked at him with approval. "Excellent idea. We can talk about the Declaration of Independence and the Constitution. You've all studied that in your social studies classes, am I correct?"

Everyone nodded. Mr. Davis seemed satisfied. "Then that will be our subject. And I hope you all will be on your best behavior Monday. Let's show Mr. Clark that we have the smartest boys and the sweetest girls in the sixth grade."

Elizabeth had to press her lips together to keep from gasping. *Sweetest* girls? Is that all they were expected to be—sweet?

"As for today," Mr. Davis continued, "I think we should spend the rest of the period talking about your big game this afternoon. I hope you boys are ready to smash the Wildcats! Now, who's pitching?"

"I'm pitching," Ross said.

"And who are your best hitters?" Mr. Davis asked.

Ross scratched his head. "Well, we've got a few. There's Ronnie and Charlie . . ." his voice faded, and he mumbled the last two names. "And Amy and Nora."

Mr. Davis frowned. "Amy and Nora? Are you telling me you have girls on this team?" When Ross nodded, Mr. Davis's frown deepened. "I certainly hope the girls aren't in key positions."

"Yeah," Charlie said. "I don't know why we let girls on the team in the first place." Several other boys nodded in agreement.

Elizabeth couldn't resist glaring furiously at the boys. Surely they remembered how Amy had won the last game for them, sliding into home half a second before the ball reached the base.

Mr. Davis was looking worried. "And this is the championship game!"

Tom raised his hand. "It's too late to change the starting lineup, Mr. Davis." He glanced anxiously at the girls. "You're not planning to play in those dresses, are you?"

Amy laughed lightly. "Of course not! I've got my uniform right here." She held up a bag. "But I'm not going to be sliding into any bases this time. I just had my uniform cleaned, and I don't want to get it dirty."

Mr. Davis shook his head wearily. The girls giggled. And Elizabeth was pleased to see the boys looking very worried.

It was the top of the seventh inning. The Tigers were leading by one run. Elizabeth knew they could have been leading by a lot more, but only the boys were scoring. The girls were concentrating on playing just the way Mr. Davis thought girls would play—badly.

Nora was on first, and Jerry McAllister was at bat. Jim Sturbridge was pitching for the Wildcats, and he sent Jerry an easy one. Jerry hit it to left field and took off. It wasn't a great hit, but it wasn't bad either. Jerry made it easily to first, and Nora should have been able to make it to second.

But instead of running normally, she took her time, prancing daintily. And by the time she got to second, the second baseman had the ball firmly clenched in his hands.

"That's the second out," Amy murmured. "Honestly, Jessica, it's harder to play badly than it is to play well. We could still win this game, you know."

"And you know what will happen then?" Jessica retorted. "The boys will still get all the credit. We're giving them exactly what they asked for. And it'll serve them right when we lose the game. Who's up at bat next?"

"I am," Amy said mournfully. She went over to home plate and picked up the bat. She took a few practice swings, the kind she was famous for—swift and powerful. Jim Sturbridge wound up the ball and threw it.

Amy chopped at the ball. "Strike one!" the umpire called.

With the second pitch, Amy acted as if she were holding a badminton racket instead of a softball bat. "Strike two!"

And with the third pitch, the bat turned into a croquet mallet—Amy was swinging two feet below the ball.

"Strike three!"

"I hated doing that," Amy confessed to Elizabeth as they made their way onto the field.

Elizabeth put a sympathetic arm around her friend. "I know," she said, "but it's for a good cause."

The boys were doing their best to keep the Wildcats from scoring. In fact, the Tigers still had a chance at winning. Jessica was in right field and Elizabeth was covering first base. But they made a big point of meeting halfway between their positions. There, they'd act as though they were having an intense conversation, and they ignore the game.

The Wildcats' best batter was up. He hit a low one to left field, and no one was able to catch it. He made it to second. The next batter hit, too—and now the Wildcats had runners on first and third.

Elizabeth imagined the boys were all breathing sighs of relief when they saw who was up next. It was Randy Mason, and he always hit high fly balls to right field that were easy to catch. Elizabeth turned and looked at Jessica. If she caught this ball, the Wildcats would be out, and the Tigers would be the sixth grade champions.

Jessica had her hands on her hips, and she was watching Randy intently. Randy swung and hit his usual high fly. It was heading straight toward Jessica. For a second, it looked as if Jessica was going to catch it. She had her hands up in the air. Then, just as the ball got closer, she covered her face protectively and made a big show of jumping out of the way.

Elizabeth turned back to Randy. He froze, as

if he couldn't believe no one had caught his ball. "Run, run!" his teammates were yelling, and he finally did. It didn't matter that someone got him out at second—the guys on first and third had come home, and the Wildcats had beaten the Tigers by two runs.

Mr. Davis, sitting in the bleachers, was blowing his whistle furiously and waving for the team to come over to him. Tom McKay caught up to Jessica and Elizabeth as they strolled toward the stands.

"Why didn't you catch that ball?" he screamed at Jessica.

Jessica smiled at him sweetly. "I was just playing like a girl." Tom scowled at her and ran on ahead. Jessica laughed gleefully.

"I'll bet they're all furious!" she said. "Now we're tied for the championship. And if they don't start treating us better, we're going to lose the final game, too!"

The team gathered around Mr. Davis. His face was red, and he looked very upset.

"That was terrible!" he yelled. "I thought you were supposed to be such a good team! And you were leading! What happened out there?"

"It was those stupid girls," Charlie said angrily. "We could have won that game easily."

"Well, you can't really blame them," Mr. Davis replied. "That's the way girls play. The real question is, why are they on the team?"

"Yeah!" yelled one of the boys, and then all of them were nodding and agreeing with Mr. Davis.

Elizabeth and Jessica looked at each other, aghast. This wasn't at all what they had expected. They thought the boys would have learned a lesson from this! Had they already forgotten that the girls were their most valuable players?

"You've still got one more chance," Mr. Davis said grimly. "And I'm going to start working with you. You know, I was a varsity baseball player in college, and I think I'm a pretty good coach." He surveyed the group with stern eyes. "We've got one entire week to practice for the final game. But there's only one way we can win." He paused and glanced meaningfully at the boys.

"We're taking all the girls off the team."

Six

The plan had backfired. Elizabeth couldn't remember ever feeling so miserable as she, Jessica, and Amy walked home from school.

"Now what are we going to do?" Amy wailed. "We're in worse shape than we were before. We don't even get to play in the final championship game."

Even though she felt as awful as Amy, Elizabeth tried to soothe her. "Come on, Amy. It's okay. So our plan didn't work. We're just going to have to come up with another one."

Amy scowled. "I just wish we could get rid of Mr. Davis. Then we'd get a new homeroom teacher, and everything could go back to normal."

"Maybe we could get him fired," Jessica suggested.

Elizabeth was shocked. "Jessica!"

"It's the only way," Jessica said. "If he's not going to leave on his own, we have to make him leave."

Amy agreed. "You know, Elizabeth, she's right. That's the only way we're going to get rid of Mr. Davis."

"But how can *we* make a teacher get fired?" Elizabeth asked. "The only person who can fire a teacher is the principal."

The girls walked in silence for a few minutes, thinking about this. Then Jessica stopped suddenly. "Hey! I've got it!"

Elizabeth turned to her sister. Jessica's eyes had lit up, and a grin spread across her face. Elizabeth knew what that look meant. Jessica had a scheme.

"Mr. Davis said that Mr. Clark is coming to our class on Monday, remember?" Jessica said, her voice bubbling with excitement. "Well, that's our chance! Mr. Clark will see what a crummy teacher Mr. Davis is, and he'll fire him!"

Amy looked doubtful. "But if the principal's in the room, you know Mr. Davis is going to try to impress him. He'll be on his best behavior."

Jessica's grin broadened. "*He* might be on his best behavior—but *we* won't! C'mon, you guys, let's hurry. We've got to call all the girls in our class. *I've* got a plan!"

Monday in homeroom, Elizabeth could feel the tension in the air. They were all about to do something they'd never done before. And Elizabeth could tell that quite a few of the other girls were feeling the same way she did—nervous. Nora was actually pale.

There were no pretty, feminine dresses to be seen. If anything, the girls were dressed more casually than usual, in jeans and T-shirts. They actually looked a little scruffy. And they weren't giggling. Today, they meant business. This was war.

Charlie and Jerry swaggered by Elizabeth's desk on their way to the boys' side of the room. Jerry spoke in an especially loud voice. "Boy, those girls play lousy softball."

"Yeah," Charlie replied, in an equally loud voice. "I'm glad we got them kicked off the team. Now we've got a chance to win."

Elizabeth ignored them. She had too many other things on her mind.

It was almost time for the bell, and the girls prepared to go into action. The girl sitting in back of Elizabeth tapped her shoulder. Elizabeth turned slightly, took the pack of chewing gum the girl held out to her, and removed a piece. Then she handed the pack across the aisle to Amy.

As the bell rang, Mr. Davis and Mr. Clark came into the room. If Mr. Davis was at all surprised by the way the girls were dressed, he didn't show it. As usual, he didn't even seem to know they were there.

"Good morning," Mr. Davis said. He began the roll call, and the girls unwrapped their sticks of gum. They began chewing noisily. As each girl's name was called, she responded with "yeah," instead of here, and punctuated the word by snapping the gum loudly.

When he finished the roll call, Mr. Davis directed his attention to the boys. "Today, as you all know, we are discussing government. Ross, what document is the basis for our democratic system?"

"The Constitution," Ross said. "I have a copy of it."

"Excellent!" Mr. Davis said. "Why don't you read the Preamble out loud."

As Ross began reciting, "We the people . . ." the girls began cracking their gum even louder. Ross could barely be heard over the din.

Mr. Davis didn't pay any attention to the unusual behavior, but Mr. Clark did. He frowned slightly and turned to the teacher just as Ross was getting to the part about "domestic tranquillity."

"Mr. Davis, do you allow students to chew gum in class?"

Mr. Davis appeared startled by the question. "Uh, no, of course not." He looked at the girls, as if he was surprised to see them there. "Would you all please get rid of that gum?"

"But we just put it in our mouths!" Jessica yelled indignantly.

"Yeah!" called Ellen. "It hasn't even lost the flavor yet!"

Mr. Davis seemed to be at a loss for words. He looked at Mr. Clark helplessly.

"Girls!" Mr. Clark barked. "Lose that gum *now*!"

Jessica touched her right eyebrow. This time, however, there were no giggles. Instead, the room echoed with a collective groan. Then the girls took the gum out of their mouths, wrapped it in the wrapper scraps—and tossed them on the floor.

Mr. Clark was aghast. "Girls! Pick those up!" He turned to Mr. Davis. "Are they always like that?"

Mr. Davis looked at him blankly. "Who?"

"The girls!" Mr. Clark exclaimed. "Do they always behave like this?"

"The girls?" Once again, Mr. Davis stared at them as if he'd never seen them before. "Uh, no, not usually. Now, class, can we get back to our discussion?"

Ross tried to find his place. "Um, 'insure domestic tranquillity—'" he began. He hadn't even gotten through one more sentence when he was interrupted by a crash. A stack of books on Nora's desk had fallen to the floor—with a little help from Nora.

"Girls, please!" Mr. Davis pleaded. "We're trying to listen to Ross. Ross, you were saying, 'insure domestic tranquillity.' Does anyone know what that means?"

None of the boys volunteered an answer, but Amy was waving her hand in the air. Mr. Davis was totally focused on the boys and didn't see her.

"Mr. Davis," Mr. Clark said, "I believe that young lady knows the answer."

"Oh," he said, finally looking at Amy. "What does 'insure domestic tranquillity' mean?"

Amy scratched her head. "Well, I'm not real sure, but I think maybe it means you should keep your house clean. You know, be domestic."

Elizabeth suppressed a giggle as Mr. Davis glared at Amy. "No, no, that's not it at all. Boys, surely one of you knows the answer to that." He called on Ronnie, but just as Ronnie started to speak, Jessica turned to Lila.

"Hey, Lila," she said loudly, "did you catch that new Johnny Buck video on TV last night?"

"Yeah," Lila replied, "wasn't it neat? He's the most gorgeous guy I've ever seen."

"Amy," Nora called from across two rows, "can you lend me a pencil?"

"Sure," Amy yelled back, sending a pencil flying across the room.

Mr. Davis was so intent on listening to Ronnie's explanation of domestic tranquillity that he didn't even notice what was going on on the girls' side. But Mr. Clark was staring at them with his mouth open. It was clear he didn't like what he saw. His face had turned beet-red.

"Girls! Girls! Be quiet!"

Mr. Davis finally turned away from the boys to see what the uproar was about. "Girls, what's going on here? Is something wrong?" he asked mildly.

"Mr. Davis!" Mr. Clark said in frustration. "Can't you keep your class under control? These girls are behaving very badly!"

Mr. Davis threw up his arms helplessly. "What can you expect from girls?"

Mr. Clark eyed him stonily. "I expect for you to demand a little discipline. This is not the way students are supposed to behave at Sweet Valley Middle School."

Mr. Davis nodded. "Yes, yes, I realize that. Now, girls, please settle down and listen to the discussion." He went back to the boys. "Who can explain the Bill of Rights to us?"

At that, several girls leaned back in their seats and closed their eyes. Others rested their chins in their hands and put on expressions of boredom. Jessica put her head on her desk and closed her eyes tightly. Then she faked a snore just to make sure Mr. Clark noticed.

Elizabeth opened one eye to see how Mr. Clark was reacting to this. He had his hands on his hips, and he was shaking his head in annoyance.

"Mr. Davis!"

"Yes?"

"The girls appear to be bored. Perhaps you should involve them in the discussion."

Mr. Davis sighed. With obvious reluctance, he went back to his desk and picked up the roll. Although he now knew who all the boys were, he hadn't bothered to learn the girls' names.

"Uh, Ellen Riteman, can you tell us what the Bill of Rights is?"

Ellen twisted a lock of her short brown hair. "No."

"Lila Fowler? What is the Bill of Rights?"

Lila stretched her arms above her head and yawned lazily. "I haven't the slightest idea."

"Can't any of you girls describe the Bill of Rights?" Mr. Davis asked.

One girl slowly raised her hand. "Is that when you buy some rights and they send you the bill?"

Mr. Davis shook his head. "No. Elizabeth Wakefield? Do you know the answer?"

Elizabeth knew what she had to do, and she couldn't let the girls down. She lifted her head. "I don't know," she said simply. "I never heard of it." Then she put her head down again.

She had a feeling that the boys were looking at her in astonishment. Elizabeth Wakefield not knowing the answer to a question—it was unbelievable!

Mr. Davis shook his head in disgust and glanced back at the roll.

"Amy Sutton, please tell us the names of the two major political parties in the United States."

Amy's forehead wrinkled as she pretended to think about this for a minute. Then she grinned. "The good guys and the bad guys?"

"This is ridiculous," Mr. Clark sputtered. "Mr. Davis, may I see you out in the hall?"

The second the two men were out the door, Jessica sprang up from her seat. She positioned herself against the wall, right next to the door, and listened intently.

She ran back to the nearest girl and gleefully reported that Mr. Clark told Mr. Davis that if he didn't get this class in shape, he would be in serious trouble!

Elizabeth leaned across her desk and shared this information with Amy. By the time Mr. Davis had returned to the room, all the girls knew.

Mr. Davis looked nervous and flustered. "I'm afraid our discussion today hasn't been very successful, and I'm disappointed in all of you. I hope some of our other projects are proceeding more smoothly. Tom, how are your rehearsals coming along?"

Tom looked at him blankly. "Rehearsals?"

"For the Sixth Grade Follies," Mr. Davis said. "Surely you've been rehearsing your skit."

"Well, uh, not exactly," Tom said.

Mr. Davis looked even more distressed. "But the program is only a few days away. Don't you think you boys ought to get moving on it? After that disastrous softball game, and today's disruption, this class had better do something right."

"The skit will be great," Ross assured him. "All we have to do is act like a bunch of apes. Besides, there aren't any girls in the skit to mess it up."

Mr. Davis sighed, then nodded. "Just do a good job, boys. All right. Listen up, everyone. I have something important to announce. The Sweet Valley Town Council is considering a proposal to remodel this school. The council members have invited a representative body of middle school students to come to their next meeting and give their opinions as to what improvements could be made. Mr. Clark has requested that each homeroom select three students."

Elizabeth and Amy exchanged excited looks. They both wanted to be part of this. Then Elizabeth's face fell. She knew Mr. Davis would never choose girls to be on the committee.

But her spirits rose when she heard his next words.

"Of course, you will want some time to think about this to decide which of your classmates would be right for such an important job. Today is

Monday: On Wednesday, we will nominate our candidates and have the election."

Everyone in class started talking at once, and Mr. Davis rapped on his desk to get their attention.

"Of course," he said, "we will want to elect our very best students." He smiled confidently at the boys, who grinned and nodded.

The bell rang, and everyone got up to leave. Elizabeth waited for Jessica.

"I want to be on that committee," Elizabeth said. "But you know what's going to happen. Only boys will be elected."

Jessica cocked her head thoughtfully. "We'll see about that." Her eyes twinkled. "It just might not work out that way at all."

Seven

◇

"I understand that the middle school is going to be remodeled," Mr. Wakefield remarked at dinner that evening.

"We heard that at school today," Elizabeth said. "And the town council wants a committee of students to come to their meeting and tell them what we need."

"Who's on the committee?" Mrs. Wakefield asked.

"We don't know yet," Jessica said. "We're going to have an election in class on Wednesday."

"It's good that they've asked for students' ideas," Mr. Wakefield noted. "After all, you kids know that school better than anyone else."

"Yeah, I'll bet Jessica's got some great ideas," Steven said as he piled the last of the coleslaw on his plate. "She'd probably ask for bigger mirrors in the girls' locker room."

Jessica wrinkled her nose at him. "I don't

even want to be on the committee. Too many meetings!"

"I've got some ideas," Elizabeth said. "We need a bigger art studio, and a darkroom for photography. And a new auditorium with a bigger stage and real lighting. And a real science laboratory. And—oh, I don't know, lots of other stuff."

Mr. Wakefield chuckled. "It sounds to me like the town council is going to get an earful from you."

Elizabeth shook her head sadly. "I doubt it. I won't even be there."

Mrs. Wakefield looked puzzled. "But you've got such interesting ideas, Elizabeth. Why don't you run for the committee?"

"You might even get two votes," Steven pointed out. "Your own, and your double's."

"She'd get more than that," Jessica assured him. "She'd get exactly ten votes—from all the girls. The problem is, there're ten boys in class, too."

"I'm sure some of the boys would vote for you, too," Mrs. Wakefield told Elizabeth.

"No way, Mom," Elizabeth replied. "The boys will vote for the boys, and the girls will vote for the girls."

"But that means the election will be tied," Mr. Wakefield said. "What happens then?"

Jessica made a face. "Mr. Davis will get to vote, and he'll break the tie."

The growl in her voice when she said "Mr. Davis" caused Mr. Wakefield to frown at her. "OK, what's wrong with *this* teacher? What's the complaint this week?"

Jessica and Elizabeth exchanged glances. "No complaints, Dad," Elizabeth said in resignation.

Their mother laughed. "Surely you're not suggesting that Mr. Davis would vote for any boy over a qualified girl?"

"Maybe," Elizabeth said in a low tone.

"Don't be silly, dear," Mrs. Wakefield said. "Teachers aren't prejudiced like that!"

"Yeah, well, they'll look for any excuse to complain about a teacher," Steven offered.

Mrs. Wakefield leaned over and patted Elizabeth's hand. "Everyone in your class knows how responsible you are, Elizabeth. If Jessica nominates you, I would bet that you'll win!"

Well, that's one bet you'd be sure to lose, Elizabeth thought. But it was no use telling her mother that. She just shrugged and said, "I'll clear the table."

Later, as she and Jessica were doing the dishes alone in the kitchen, Elizabeth was free to complain all she wanted to. "It's not fair! I really want to be on that committee, and so does Amy. But we don't have a chance!"

"You know," Jessica said, "if one of the boys doesn't show up on Wednesday, the girls would have the majority. And Mr. Davis wouldn't even get to vote."

"That's true," Elizabeth said. "But how do we know if someone's going to be absent? And, anyway, what if one of the girls gets sick?"

"There must be some way to get a boy to stay home," Jessica mused. "And it only has to be one boy."

"But, Jess, there's no way we can keep a boy out of class. Unless—" She paused and then giggled. "Unless we kidnap one of them, tie him up, and not let him go 'til after the bell."

Jessica looked thoughtful. "That's not a bad idea."

"Jessica!"

"Just kidding, just kidding," Jessica added hastily. "But there must be a way. . . ."

"What's most depressing about all this is that a majority of the boys probably don't even want to be on the committee."

Jessica nodded in agreement. "Yeah, it's too much work for them."

"And some of them would be too chicken to get up in front of the town council," Elizabeth said. "I mean, that could be pretty scary, talking to a bunch of adults. It wouldn't bother me, of course, but can you imagine someone like—like Ricky Capaldo?"

The thought of the shyest person in the entire sixth grade standing up in front of the town council made Jessica roll her eyes. "He'd die! He'd absolutely fall apart!"

"But if he gets nominated, he'll win," Elizabeth said. "And just because he's a boy. Jessica, hand me that sponge and I'll wipe the counter."

When her twin didn't respond, she looked at her in alarm. Jessica was standing very still with her mouth slightly open.

"Jessica! What's the matter?" Then she saw the familiar glint in her sister's eyes.

"That's perfect, Lizzie," Jessica squealed. "Ricky Capaldo!"

"What are you talking about?" Elizabeth asked her in bewilderment.

"That committee's going to be all girls! I've got a plan!"

"You girls are off to an early start," Mrs. Wakefield said the next morning.

Elizabeth gulped down her orange juice, while Jessica grabbed a slice of toast with one hand and her notebook with the other. "We want to get to school early," Elizabeth explained, setting her glass down. "There's someone we have to see."

Without offering any further explanation, the girls yelled good-bye and ran out the door.

"If we hurry, we're sure to get to school early enough to find Ricky alone," Elizabeth noted.

"He's always the first person in the homeroom because his father drops him off on his way to work."

On their way to school, they rehearsed what they were going to say to Ricky. By the time they entered the practically deserted building, they knew their parts by heart. They walked quietly to their homeroom, and Elizabeth peeked in the doorway.

"He's there," she whispered. "He's in his seat, reading. And he's all alone. Okay, Jess, go to it."

Jessica tossed her head and strolled casually into the classroom. Elizabeth stayed out in the hall, but she edged closer to the door so she could hear the conversation.

"Hi, Ricky," Jessica said. "What are you reading?"

Ricky turned a little pink. He was particularly shy around girls. "Uh, it's a book," he mumbled.

"That's nice," Jessica said. "Isn't it exciting about the committee elections?"

"Uh, yeah, I guess so."

Jessica perched on the desk across from his. "You know, Ricky, I was thinking that you'd be good on that committee. I'll bet you've got lots of good ideas about remodeling the school."

Ricky looked startled. "No, I don't."

"Oh, you're just being modest," Jessica said

sweetly. "I know you'd be absolutely perfect on that committee. In fact, I'm planning to nominate you myself."

Now Ricky looked horrified. "I—I don't want to be on the committee."

Jessica laughed merrily. "Don't be silly! Of course you do! And I'm sure you'll be elected. All the boys will vote for you, and I'm going to get all the girls to vote for you, too."

With that, she smiled brightly, got off the desk, and walked out. She didn't have to look back to know what Ricky's expression was. She could just imagine the look of terror on his face.

Back in the hall, she beamed triumphantly at Elizabeth. "I've done my part! Now it's your turn."

Elizabeth walked into the room. "Hi, Ricky," she said casually. She gazed at him in concern. "What's the matter? You look kind of upset."

He just shrugged and didn't say anything, so Elizabeth tried again. "Did you just get some bad news or something?"

Finally, Ricky nodded. "J-Jessica was just in here. She said she's going to nominate me for that committee."

"That's nice," Elizabeth said.

Ricky shook his head. "No, it's not," he said in a small voice. "I don't want to be on it."

Elizabeth tried to look sympathetic. "Gee, that's too bad. If Jessica nominates you, you know you'll be elected. And then you'd have to tell Mr. Davis you don't want to be on the committee. I guess that would be pretty embarrassing."

Ricky nodded fervently. "Maybe, uh, maybe you could tell Jessica not to do it."

Elizabeth smiled helplessly. "I don't think that would work, Ricky. Once Jessica's made up her mind to do something, there's no stopping her."

Ricky stared down at his desk.

"Of course," Elizabeth added, "if you're not in school tomorrow, she couldn't nominate you, could she?" Now Ricky looked up, and there was hope in his eyes.

Kids were starting to come into the room, and Elizabeth went to her own seat. Jessica came back in and looked at Elizabeth with her eyebrows raised. Elizabeth grinned and nodded.

When the bell rang on Wednesday morning, Elizabeth looked around to the boys' side of the room and counted. There were only nine. She sighed in relief. Their scheme had worked! She turned to flash Jessica a "V for victory" sign, and then her face fell.

There was an empty seat next to Jessica. Lila Fowler was absent, too.

Elizabeth sank deeper in her seat, filled with disappointment. They were right back where they had started from, with an even number of boys and girls. And Mr. Davis would get to break the tie.

Mr. Davis called the roll, noting the absences of Ricky and Lila. "All right, class," he began, "as I told you on Monday, we need to elect our representatives to the town council. The floor is now open for nominations."

Amy jumped out of her seat. "I'd like to nominate Elizabeth Wakefield."

What's the point, Elizabeth thought grimly. *There's no way I'm going to win.*

Mr. Davis wrote Elizabeth's name on the board, then looked at the boys' side. "More nominations?"

The boys looked at one another uneasily. As Elizabeth suspected, none of them were too eager to get involved. For a moment, she felt a spark of hope. Maybe, if none of the boys were nominated, girls could get on the committee after all. She held up her hand, and since she was the only person in the room with her hand up, Mr. Davis was forced to call on her.

"I nominate Amy Sutton," she said.

Mr. Davis looked at her kindly. "Now, I want all you girls to think long and hard before you nominate one another. Remember, this is an extremely important committee, and you'll be expected to work very hard. A job like this requires firm and decisive action."

Elizabeth repeated what she had said. "I nominate Amy Sutton."

Mr. Davis shook his head regretfully, but he wrote Amy's name on the board. He turned to the boys hopefully. "Let's have some more nominations."

Still, the boys didn't move, and again Elizabeth waved her hand in the air. There was no law that said you couldn't nominate two people. "Nora Mercandy," she called out.

Mr. Davis glared at her with annoyance. He went back to the board, scrawled Nora's name quickly, and looked at the boys, his eyes pleading.

"Boys, are you going to let this happen? This committee could affect everything that happens here at Sweet Valley Middle School. You could help the school get a bigger gym, or even a new science lab! Come on, boys! We need some *men* on this committee!"

That finally stirred them to action. Charlie nominated Jerry, Jerry nominated Charlie, and Tom nominated Ronnie. Elizabeth and Amy looked at each other in despair.

"Very good," Mr. Davis said, looking relieved. "We've got six candidates, and we need to elect three. If, by any chance, the votes are tied, I will cast the deciding vote. Now, for the first candidate, Jerry McAllister."

But before he could say "all in favor," the door

to the room opened, and in walked Lila. "Sorry I'm late," she said to Mr. Davis. "Here's my excuse." She tossed a folded piece of paper on his desk and ran to her seat.

Elizabeth had never been so happy to see Lila in her life. All over her side of the room, girls were sitting up straighter and murmuring excitedly.

"Attention, please!" Mr. Davis didn't look happy at all. "We have to vote. And, girls, remember, you don't just want to vote for your friends. You want to vote for the most-qualified people."

Which is exactly what Elizabeth wanted them to do. And when the hands were counted, Charlie, Jerry, and Ronnie each got nine "in favor" votes; Elizabeth, Amy, and Nora each got ten.

Cheers erupted on the girls' side of the room. From the boys' side came hisses and boos. Mr. Davis, looking aghast, pounded on his desk for order. Then the bell rang.

"This is fantastic!" Amy declared as she joined Elizabeth and Nora in the hall.

"Fantastic," Elizabeth echoed happily. Only Nora didn't look terribly enthusiastic.

"You know," she said slowly, "in a way, it's too bad it has to be this way. I mean, Ronnie would have been good on that committee—probably better than I."

"You'll do fine," Elizabeth assured her, but in

the back of her mind, she agreed with Nora. Ronnie would have been good.

But this was war. And the girls had finally won a battle.

Eight

◇

That afternoon, as Elizabeth and Amy were leaving their last class, Elizabeth remembered something. "With all the excitement about the election today, I forgot all about the Follies."

"Me, too," Amy said. "And it's tomorrow. I wonder what it's going to be like?"

"Not too great, I'll bet," Elizabeth replied. "It sounds like such a dippy story. And Tom doesn't know anything about directing."

They were walking toward the exit when Jessica came running up to them. "Listen, you guys," she said, "I just found out that the boys are rehearsing for the Follies in the cafeteria. Let's go watch them!"

The prospect didn't thrill Elizabeth. She had a feeling she'd just get depressed watching the boys practice when she wasn't involved at all. "What's the point?" she asked.

"Oh, c'mon," Jessica urged. "It'll be fun! We can laugh at them."

"*I'd* like to see what's going on," Amy admitted. "After all, they *are* going to be representing our entire homeroom. Let's do it."

Reluctantly, Elizabeth agreed, and the girls headed to the cafeteria. As they approached, they could hear the boys yelling and making all kinds of noise.

They peeked inside and were greeted by total chaos. Tables had been pushed aside to create an empty space toward the front of the room. Charlie, Jerry, and three other boys were running back and forth, making loud grunting noises. Ronnie was holding a yardstick as if it were a rifle, and he was pointing it at Ross. "Pow, pow," he yelled.

"Ha! You missed me!" Ross shouted back.

Poor Tom just stared at them, looking totally frustrated and confused. "C'mon, we gotta get to work!" he yelled, but the boys ignored him.

"They look like first graders at recess," Elizabeth whispered to Amy. The girls slipped inside and sat down in the back of the room.

Finally, the boys settled down, and Tom wearily ran his hand through his hair. "Let's start from the beginning," he said. "Ross, you're the real ape. You come on first."

Ross lumbered into the center of the space, his arms up in the air and held out sideways. He took big, clumping steps, and with each step he shouted, "Ugh! Ugh!"

"That's not how an ape moves," Ronnie objected. "He's acting like the monster in *Franken-stein*."

Ross immediately stopped doing his imitations. "Oh, yeah? What do *you* know about apes?"

"We just saw some in the zoo last week," Ronnie said. "And that's not how they looked."

"That how they looked to *me*," Ross insisted. He turned to Tom. "Isn't this right?" He raised his arms again.

"I don't know," Tom said. "I guess it's OK." He consulted the script in his hand. "It says here you're supposed to beat your chest and make noises like an ape."

Ross began pounding on his chest and screeching, but Elizabeth thought he sounded more like a very sick dog than an ape. She could tell from Tom's expression that he wasn't too pleased, either.

"That doesn't sound right," he said.

Ross scowled. "Then show me how you want me to do it."

Tom scratched his head and looked helpless. "I guess it's OK. Now you're supposed to run off the stage."

"Which way?" Ross asked.

"I don't care," Tom replied. "Just get off the stage. Now Ronnie and the rest of you guys come on."

The other boys ambled into the center area and stood there uncomfortably. "What do we do?" Ronnie asked.

"You're supposed to be hunters," Tom said. "Act like hunters."

"How do hunters act?" Charlie asked.

"I don't know," Tom snapped. "Jerry, you're supposed to say something."

"What am I supposed to say?"

Tom looked as if he was going to explode. "Didn't you learn your lines?"

Jerry shrugged. "I guess I forgot."

In the back of the cafeteria, Elizabeth had her hands over her eyes, Amy was groaning, and Jessica had her mouth covered so the boys wouldn't hear her giggles.

"This is *awful*," Amy exclaimed.

"I can't bear to watch it," Elizabeth said. "It's going to be so embarrassing when they get on that stage tomorrow."

"Uh-oh," Jessica said suddenly. "We've been spotted."

Sure enough, Tom was looking in their direction. The girls saw him beckon Ronnie over, and they had a whispered consultation. Then Tom turned abruptly and started toward the girls.

"Should we make a run for it?" Amy asked.

"No, let's wait and see what he has to say," Elizabeth said. As Tom approached, she could see he didn't look angry—just frustrated. When he spoke, he directed his remarks to her.

"I'm having some problems with this skit," he told her.

"So I see," Elizabeth replied. "I guess you've never directed a play before."

"Well, no, not exactly." He paused, as if he was trying to get up some nerve before he spoke again. When he did, his words came out in a rush. "Do you think you could help us?"

"Help you how?"

"Show us what to do, where to stand, stuff like that."

Elizabeth knew exactly what he wanted. "You mean, you want me to direct it for you."

"Not exactly. You could be the assistant director."

Elizabeth's eyes widened, and she batted her lashes. "But, Tom, I'm sure Mr. Davis wouldn't approve of my being assistant director."

Tom shifted uneasily. "Well, he doesn't have to know, does he? We don't have to tell him you helped."

Elizabeth almost felt sorry for him. Almost—but not quite. She shook her head.

At first, Tom looked dismayed. Then his expression switched to anger. "I think you're being pretty selfish," he stated. "Don't you care how our homeroom looks in front of the whole school?"

Of course she cared. And she knew she could help Tom make the skit better. For a few seconds, she thought she just might give in. After all, it was for the good of the class.

But Jessica and Amy were there, watching her. If she helped Tom, she'd be a traitor to their cause.

Elizabeth faced Tom squarely. "Forget it! You boys didn't want us to have any part of this. And I'm not going to help you now."

Tom's face went red. "You know what you are, Elizabeth? You're jealous! Just because I got to be the director and you didn't!"

Elizabeth couldn't think of a good comeback to that. "Oh yeah?" was all she could manage.

"Yeah!" was Tom's snappy retort.

By now, the rest of the boys had gathered around them. "Hey, Tom," Charlie called to him, "you're not asking dumb girls for help, are you?"

Jerry sneered at them. "What are they doing here, anyway? We don't need them hanging around."

Tom caught the spirit. "Yeah, they messed up our softball game. They don't have to mess up our skit, too."

"You won't need any help with that," Jessica shot back. "You're doing a great job messing up all by yourselves. C'mon, girls, let's get out of here."

"Good riddance!" one of the boys yelled after them.

Elizabeth's eyes were flashing with anger, as the girls walked rapidly down the hall toward the door. It seemed like only yesterday that she and

Tom had been talking, joking, and laughing. And now they'd probably never speak to each other again.

"Maybe I should have helped him," she murmured softly.

"Are you crazy?" Jessica shook her head violently. "No way, Lizzie."

"She's right," Amy told Elizabeth gently. "I know you feel bad about Tom. But we have to make the boys realize that Mr. Davis is wrong about girls. And this is the only way."

Elizabeth hoped they were right. And she also hoped this wasn't going to go on much longer.

The next morning, instead of going to their homeroom, Elizabeth and Jessica went directly to the auditorium where the whole school had gathered.

"There's Mr. Davis," Jessica said.

Elizabeth shuddered. "Let's sit as far away from him as possible."

The other girls in their class must have had the same idea. Elizabeth and Jessica found them sitting together on the opposite side of the room.

"How bad is our skit going to be?" one girl wondered out loud.

"Pretty bad," Elizabeth told her.

The vice principal, Mr. Edwards, went up onto the stage and spoke into a microphone. "Welcome to the Sixth Grade Follies. As you all know, this is an annual tradition here at Sweet Valley Middle School. Each of our sixth-grade homerooms has prepared an original skit. After each presentation, your applause will be measured on a special applause meter, and when the program is over, I'll announce the winner. And now—on with the show!"

The first skit was extremely clever. A girl with long blond hair tied back with a blue ribbon wandered onto the stage. "The funniest thing just happened to me," she said. "I was chasing a rabbit, and I fell down the rabbit hole. When I got to the bottom, I found myself here, at some strange place called Sweet Valley Middle School."

What followed was a cute takeoff on *Alice in Wonderland*. The Cheshire cat was the principal, the Mad Hatter was the librarian, and the tea party was a typical cafeteria lunchroom scene. The audience was laughing so hard that Elizabeth could barely hear some of the lines, but the ones she heard were funny. She would have been laughing along with the rest of them if she hadn't been thinking how awful her homeroom's skit was going to look in comparison.

When the skit was over, the audience applauded enthusiastically, and then settled down for the next performance.

The second skit was good, too. It was about a football team with a mysterious player who never took his helmet off. He scored all the touchdowns, and he was the team hero, but no one knew who he was. At the end, his helmet fell off—and the star of the team turned out to be a girl.

"I wonder if Mr. Davis understood that," Jessica whispered to Elizabeth.

"I doubt it," Elizabeth replied. Along with the rest of the audience, she applauded the skit vigorously.

And then came their homeroom's skit. When Tom came onstage wearing a rubber gorilla mask, there were a few titters in the audience. But that was the last laugh the skit got.

It was awful, even worse than it had seemed the day before. The boys were running all over the stage, bumping into one another. Most of them forgot their lines, and the ones who remembered theirs couldn't even be heard from behind their masks. No one could figure out what was going on.

Some kids in the audience started booing. Elizabeth bowed her head in shame. When the skit was over, there was hardly any applause at all.

When all the skits had been performed, and the awards presented, the girls stayed in their seats while everyone else stood up and headed for their next class.

"I don't want to face anyone," Nora moaned. "I feel like hiding for the rest of the day."

On her way out, Elizabeth passed Mr. Clark

and Mr. Edwards. She couldn't help hearing what Mr. Clark was saying.

"I don't understand what's happened to that class. They seem completely out of control. If they don't shape up, I'm afraid I'm going to have to do something about Mr. Davis."

Good, Elizabeth thought. She hoped Mr. Clark would speak to Mr. Davis. And she knew exactly what she wanted Mr. Clark to say:

"Mr. Davis, you're fired."

Nine

◇

Mr. Davis made a speech in homeroom on Friday morning. As he spoke, he fiddled with his tie, and he shifted his weight from one foot to the other. Elizabeth could see he was very nervous.

"Our principal, Mr. Clark, was not happy about your Follies presentation yesterday. He felt the performance showed poor planning and organization. I must say I agree with him."

For once, he wasn't looking directly at the boys. Instead, his eyes seemed to be focused on the wall opposite him, as if he didn't want to meet anyone's eyes.

"Um, Mr. Clark also wanted to know why none of the girls were involved in the skit."

All over the girls' side of the room, meaningful glances were exchanged. Mr. Davis paused, struggling for words.

"Perhaps . . . perhaps girls should have been involved. After all, it was supposed to be a theatrical performance. And girls can be very talented when it comes to acting."

Elizabeth couldn't believe what she was hearing. Was Mr. Davis about to apologize? Were the girls about to become equal members of this sixthgrade homeroom? She watched Mr. Davis expectantly, eyes alert, hope growing in her heart.

Mr. Davis spoke slowly. "As you may know, my background is only in all-boys schools—mostly military academies. I have never taught girls before. I admit that I have limited experience with them and with their talents and abilities. Perhaps I have been too narrow in my beliefs."

He stopped, then took a deep breath before he went on. "The skit may have been a good opportunity to include girls in a classroom activity; however, it is too late for regrets. In the future, I will try to include more girls in activities that are suitable for them."

Elizabeth looked at Amy. "What a relief," she murmured.

Amy nodded fervently. "No kidding," she whispered. She raised her hand. "Does this mean we're back on the softball team?"

To Elizabeth's surprise, Mr. Davis's face suddenly became hard and stern. "No. I was only referring to *suitable* activities. I realize that physical exercise is good for girls as well as boys, but this is a championship game—and we must win it. It's the only way this homeroom can rise above yesterday's Follies disaster." His expression softened, and his next words were spoken kindly.

"Look, girls. It is important to all of us that we win this game, right? Well, when it comes to athletics, boys are simply better suited than girls. It's a fact of nature that no one can change. I'm sorry, but maybe you can play next time when it's less crucial."

It was as if a big black cloud had suddenly appeared over one side of the classroom. Their brief moment of triumph had vanished, leaving behind only despair. The girls hadn't won, after all. They *still* weren't equal.

When the bell rang, Elizabeth motioned for Jessica and Amy and Nora to meet her in the hallway. The girls gathered just outside the door.

"Do you have your uniforms here at school?" Elizabeth asked them. The girls nodded.

"Mine's in the gym locker," Jessica said.

"Mine's there too," Nora said. "I brought it this morning. I thought maybe Mr. Davis might change his mind and let us play, after all." She sighed mournfully. "I guess it's just going to sit in that locker forever."

"I'm not even going to the stupid game," Amy growled.

"Yes, you are," Elizabeth stated firmly. "We all are. And we're going to wear our uniforms."

"What's the point?" Amy asked.

"It's the championship game," Elizabeth said. "And I'm sure Mr. Clark is going to be there. Practically the whole school will be there. And I want them to see us, in our uniforms, just sitting there in the stands. Let them know the girls are supposed to be on the team, and it's Mr. Davis's fault that we're not playing. Let the whole world see that the girls in Mr. Davis's homeroom are not considered equal!"

The bleachers were packed. All of Sweet Valley Middle School had turned out to see the big game. But the stands were unusually quiet for such an important event. There wasn't much to cheer about.

There had been no scoring at all in the first inning. Elizabeth sat with the other girls in her class and watched the players with her elbows on her knees and her chin in her hands. All sorts of feelings were churning inside her. She felt frustrated as she watched some of the weaker players make mistakes. She was angry at not being able to play herself. And deep in her heart, she felt sympathy for the team, which was bound to lose.

"I would have made it to third base," Nora said sadly as some particularly slow runner failed to reach second before the ball did.

"That was an easy pitch," Amy remarked a few seconds later as one of the boys struck out. "I could have slammed it out of the park."

In the bottom of the second inning, the Wildcats were up, and the batter hit a fly ball. It was headed straight for Tom in the outfield and it looked as though he was going to catch it. But he fumbled and dropped the ball, giving the Wildcats a chance to score.

"Look at Mr. Davis," Jessica said to Elizabeth. Elizabeth turned around to see the teacher, who was sitting right behind them. His face was blazing, and he looked furious.

"Tom's in trouble," Elizabeth murmured. Sure enough, as soon as the inning was over, Mr. Davis beckoned the boys over to the stands. When the boys were all there, he started yelling so loudly that Elizabeth flinched. At first he criticized them all in general; then he focused his anger on Tom.

"What's the matter with you? You caught that ball like a girl!"

Tom's face was almost as red as Mr. Davis's, but it wasn't from anger. Elizabeth knew Tom well enough to realize that he was ashamed and embarrassed, twice over—once for playing badly, and again for being yelled at in public. And despite her own lingering anger at Tom, Elizabeth couldn't help feeling sorry for him.

"What?" Jessica sputtered. "So that's how he thinks a girl catches. I could show him a thing or two."

Two kids in front of them got up. "This game is boring," one of them said.

"Yeah, let's go," the other said. "I don't get it. I thought this team was supposed to be good."

"Hey, Jessica!" called a voice from behind them.

Jessica turned and waved to a group of Unicorns sitting up in the bleachers. Janet Howell, the president, leaned over toward her.

"How come you're not playing?" Janet asked. "I thought you were the hotshot in the outfield."

"I *am*," Jessica replied. "But Mr. Davis won't let the girls play. He thinks girls aren't good enough for championship softball."

All the girls turned to see Janet's reaction to that statement. The older girl's mouth dropped open, and her eyes flashed. "I can't believe that! Is he crazy?" She was answered by a row of bobbing heads.

The game continued, and things got worse and worse. The Wildcats managed to bring another player home, and now the score was two to nothing. Humiliation and despair settled in around Elizabeth. By the fourth inning, more people were leaving the stands.

Jessica couldn't take it any longer. She got up.

"You're not leaving, are you?" Elizabeth asked.

Jessica didn't reply. She climbed to the next level, and Elizabeth watched her huddle with the seventh- and eighth-grade Unicorns sitting there. When the conversation was finished, the girls separated and began moving through the stands, talking to the kids on the bleachers.

The Unicorns were fast workers. Within a few minutes, the bleachers echoed with a resounding chant: "We want the girls! We want the girls!"

Elizabeth saw Tom at the foot of the stands, looking up at the yelling crowd with a thoughtful expression. Ronnie and Charlie joined him. They had gathered right under her nose, and she could hear every word.

"Listen to those jerks," Charlie jeered. "What do they know?"

Tom shook his head. "The crowd's right. We need the girls. We're never going to win this game without them."

Charlie looked at him as if he'd lost his mind. "Are you nuts, or something? Don't you remember how they played last week?"

Tom turned to the bleachers, looking directly at Elizabeth. "You guys were doing that on purpose, right? To teach us a lesson?"

Elizabeth nodded. "Mr. Davis was acting as if we girls were so inferior. And you guys were going along with that. So we decided to act just the way we were being treated."

Tom studied the ground for a minute. When his head came up, he wore a shamefaced expression. "I knew it all along."

"Well, maybe it's not too late," Ronnie interjected. "C'mon, girls, we can still win this game."

"All-*right!*" Amy shouted gleefully. She jumped up, and Jessica and Nora followed. But Elizabeth stopped them.

"Hold on," she said, turning to the boys. "No, guys, we're not going to play."

"What?" Nora exclaimed.

Elizabeth went on, her voice quiet but firm. "Letting us play this game isn't enough. Everything in homeroom has to change. We deserve to be treated like equal citizens in that class. No more pushing us around. We're not playing this game unless we're guaranteed everything will go back to normal."

Tom and Ronnie looked at each other. "We agree," they said quickly. Elizabeth glared at Charlie, who was watching them all in disbelief.

"Yeah, it's OK with me, too," he said finally. "Now, let's get out there and play."

"Not so fast," Elizabeth said. "We want a guarantee from Mr. Davis, too."

Elizabeth followed Tom's eyes to Mr. Davis. The teacher was staring into space, his expression stern. Elizabeth figured he must be nervous. Losing this game wouldn't make Mr. Clark any happier with him.

Tom steeled himself. "It's worth a try," he muttered and headed toward Mr. Davis.

Ronnie turned to Elizabeth and the other

girls. "You know," he said, "most of the guys don't like what's been going on in homeroom, either."

"*I* do," Charlie interjected.

But Ronnie ignored him and continued. "I mean, for a while, it was cool being in charge and all that. But it wasn't fair, either." He paused, then added shyly, "And besides, we kind of missed hanging out with you."

"*I* didn't," Charlie said.

The cries of "we want the girls, we want the girls," were getting louder and louder. The girls strained to hear what Tom was saying to Mr. Davis, but it was impossible. They could see the teacher's expression, though. His mouth was set in a thin line, and he was shaking his head. Tom wasn't giving up, though.

"He stopped shaking his head," Amy said suddenly.

"He's getting up!" Jessica added.

Elizabeth held her breath as Mr. Davis slowly made his way over to them. And she didn't exhale until he was standing directly in front of them.

He could barely meet their eyes as he spoke. "The boys seem to think you girls can save this game." His expression told them that he didn't believe what he said, but he was just too tired to argue any longer. "You have my permission to play."

The girls didn't move. Mr. Davis seemed surprised. "Well, isn't that what you wanted?"

"It's not enough," Elizabeth said firmly. "Mr. Davis, you've been treating us like second-class citizens ever since you came here. We don't think it's fair, and we won't take it any longer."

Mr. Davis glanced anxiously at the playing field. The Wildcats were spreading out into position.

"OK, OK," he said hurriedly. "Whatever you want. Now get out there."

Still, the girls didn't move, and Jessica spoke. "First of all, Mr. Davis, you owe us an apology for the way you've treated us."

Mr. Davis was taken aback. "Excuse me, young lady, but teachers do not apologize to students."

Amy's eyes narrowed. "Why not, if they're wrong? My parents would."

Elizabeth couldn't believe they were actually talking like this to a teacher! But Mr. Davis was listening and seemed to be deep in thought. Finally, he shook his head and there was the trace of a smile on his lips.

"All right," he said. "I apologize. *Now* will you get out there?"

On the field, the umpire blew his whistle, and Elizabeth turned to the others.

"C'mon, girls! Let's play ball!"

Ten

$\diamond$

It was a whole new ball game. It was as if a burden had been lifted from the shoulders of the players. Everyone seemed to come back to life.

The boys were inspired by the presence of the girls. And the girls were ready to play. When the Tigers were up, Nora took her turn at bat. She couldn't hit the ball, but she walked and managed to get on first. Ricky Capaldo was up next. Normally, he either walked or was struck out. But the mood of the game must have touched him, and today he put out that extra effort. He hit the ball far enough to put him on first; and Nora, the fastest runner in the class, made it to third.

Amy was next up at bat. Waiting on the sidelines, Elizabeth could see the tension in the eyes of the pitcher. Everyone knew what Amy was capable of doing. But could she do it today?

The pitch came. Amy swung. The ball went sailing into the sky. And it kept on going, beyond the reach of anyone in the field. Nora came home, Ricky came home, and Amy ran around the diamond like lightning. She could have skipped if she'd wanted to, or even strolled—there was no way that ball would come home before she did.

Now the score was three to two, and the crowd was going wild. Elizabeth jumped up and down and looked all around her. She glimpsed a variety of expressions—excitement in the stands, glee among the Tigers, stunned surprise from Mr. Davis, and panic on the faces of the Wildcats.

The Wildcats were caught unprepared. They had expected another easy victory, like last week's. Frantically, they tried to gather some momentum, but there was no way their efforts could match the enthusiasm of the Tigers. In the next inning they didn't score at all.

But their defenses were up, and in the top of the seventh they fought back hard. Tom, who would be pitching in the bottom of the inning, studied the Wildcat pitcher carefully.

"Look at the way he's got his hand curved," he said to Elizabeth. "I think I can do that."

"Sure you can," Elizabeth said encouragingly. "You're the best pitcher we have!" The brief conversation filled her with happiness. It felt so good to be talking to Tom again!

The Tigers weren't able to score in the seventh inning. But at least now they were in the lead, and if they could keep the Wildcats from scoring in the bottom of the seventh, the championship would be theirs.

Elizabeth took her position on first. She watched Tom approach the pitcher's mound, his expression intense and serious as he rolled the ball around in his hands. Briefly, he turned his head and winked at Elizabeth. She smiled back at him with all the confidence she could muster and gave him a thumbs-up sign.

Tom fixed steely eyes on the batter and held them there for a few seconds. Then he wound up and threw.

Elizabeth gasped. It was a perfect imitation of the Wildcat pitcher's curve. Before long the Wildcats had suffered their first out.

The next batter was ready for him, though. Somehow, he managed to make contact with Tom's curve ball and got himself on first.

The next batter wasn't quite so prepared. She had two strikes against her before she finally hit. Now the Wildcats had players on first and second, and Elizabeth started to get really nervous when she saw who was up next.

It was Aaron Dallas, the biggest kid in the sixth grade, and the most powerful batter. He could hit *anything*. And he usually hit to right field. Elizabeth turned to look at Jessica.

This was it—the big moment. Tom wound up,

pitched the ball, and there was a resounding smack as Aaron's bat met it.

It was a long hit, straight out to right field. Jessica rushed forward to meet it, scooped it off the ground, and shot it to Elizabeth on first. Elizabeth didn't even have time to think—she immediately whipped it out to Ross on second.

And the game was over! Elizabeth was immediately swept up with the rest of her classmates in one gigantic hug.

Everyone agreed that it was Jessica's fielding that had saved the game, and a couple of boys hoisted her up on their shoulders. The team surged forward toward the stands, chanting "We're number one! We're number one!"

Mr. Davis was waiting for them. His expression was a combination of relief, admiration, and bewilderment.

"Well," he said, as the boys lowered Jessica to the ground, "that was some game!"

"What did you think of Jessica's play in right field?" Tom asked him.

Mr. Davis shook his head in amazement. "I have to admit, she threw it like—like—"

"Like a girl?" Elizabeth asked mischievously.

Everyone laughed, but Jessica was studying Mr. Davis thoughtfully. "You don't know much about girls at all, do you?" she asked.

Mr. Davis was silent for a few seconds. "No, I

guess I don't," he said finally. "And I've got some thinking to do."

"About what?" Jessica asked.

Mr. Davis smiled. "About my attitudes. I got off to a pretty bad start with you kids. But if you'll give me another chance, I know that it's going to change. How about it. Can we start all over?"

The kids looked at one another.

"Can we go back to our old seats?" Nora asked.

"Absolutely."

"And no more treating girls differently from boys?" Amy asked.

Mr. Davis nodded. "I promise. And to get things off to the right start, how about letting me treat you all to a celebration? Pizza, anyone?"

The sixth graders let out a whoop. As Mr. Davis led them off the playing field, Elizabeth had a feeling that a new day had arrived. The girls were back in the ball game—for good.

Eleven

◇

On Sunday morning, Jessica and Elizabeth were in the kitchen making sandwiches. Only this time, they weren't complaining about it.

"We haven't had a family picnic in ages," Elizabeth said happily as she spread mayonnaise on a slice of bread. Then she added layers of lettuce, tomato, and cold chicken.

"How many sandwiches do you think we should make?" Jessica asked, carefully cutting a bright red tomato into thick, juicy slices.

"It's just the five of us," Elizabeth said. She took a large covered bowl of potato salad from the refrigerator and placed it in the cooler on the kitchen table.

Jessica washed another tomato in the sink. "Then we need one each for you, me, Dad, and Mom, and five for Steven."

Elizabeth laughed. "C'mon, Jess, he couldn't eat *five*!" Then she paused. "Well, he probably *could*, but Mom won't let him!" She glanced out the window. "It's perfect picnic weather. Secca Lake's going to be beautiful today."

Jessica smiled dreamily. "Remember the last time we were there? I saw some really cute guys throwing Frisbees. I wonder if they go there every Sunday?"

Elizabeth rolled her eyes. "Honestly, Jessica, is that all you can think of? Boys, boys, boys."

"I think about other things, too," Jessica declared. "Like clothes. Besides, *you* think about boys, too. Aren't you happier at school now that the boys and the girls are speaking to one another again?"

Elizabeth had to admit that Jessica was right. "I'm glad everything's back to normal. To tell the truth, I didn't really want Mr. Davis to leave or be fired. I just wanted him to stop acting like such a creep."

"Who's acting like a creep?" Steven sauntered into the kitchen. "Not me, of course."

"And not Mr. Davis, either," Elizabeth said cheerfully. "We finally convinced him that girls and boys are equal."

"How did you do that?" Steven asked. "Hypnotize him?" He examined the contents of the cooler. "You'd better be making lots of sandwiches. Eating outside makes me twice as hungry."

"Eating anywhere makes you twice as hungry," Jessica retorted. "Where're Mom and Dad?"

"Upstairs," Steven replied. He started out of the room, but Jessica stopped him.

"Carry the cooler out to the car," she instructed him.

Steven grinned. "Why me? If you girls are so equal, you should be strong enough to carry it yourselves."

"Steven!" the twins groaned in unison.

"OK, OK," Steven said with a grin. "I'm out of here."

He had just left the kitchen with the cooler when Mr. Wakefield appeared at the door. "Are you girls ready to go?" he asked. He was smiling, but his forehead was puckered.

"Just about," Elizabeth said. "Where's Mom?"

"She's not coming with us."

"Not coming!" Jessica exclaimed. "Why not?"

"Your mother's not feeling well," Mr. Wakefield said. "It's probably just a little cold, but she thinks she'd better stay in bed today."

Elizabeth was surprised. Her mother was hardly ever sick—and even when she was, she didn't stay in bed.

Mr. Wakefield sensed the concern in her expression. "Don't worry," he said. "I'm sure she'll be fine by tomorrow." But even as he said this, something in his eyes told Elizabeth he was worried.

"I left my sunglasses upstairs," Jessica said.

"I'll get them," Elizabeth offered. She ran upstairs, got the sunglasses from Jessica's room, and then paused by her parents' bedroom. The door was slightly open, and she peeked inside.

Her mother was sleeping. Elizabeth tiptoed in to get a look at her. Studying her mother's face, she had a feeling she knew why her father seemed disturbed. Mrs. Wakefield's face was pale, and there were dark shadows around her eyes.

Something was wrong. Her mother didn't look well at all. And she definitely didn't look like someone who would be fine by tomorrow.

Is Mrs. Wakefield seriously ill? Find out in Sweet Valley Twins 18, **CENTRE OF ATTENTION.**

We hope you enjoyed reading this book. If you would like to receive further information about available titles in the Bantam series, just write to the address below, with your name and address: Kim Prior, Bantam Books, 61–63 Uxbridge Road, Ealing, London W5 5SA.

If you live in Australia or New Zealand and would like more information about the series, please write to:

Sally Porter
Transworld Publishers
(Australia) Pty Ltd
15–23 Helles Avenue
Moorebank
NSW 2170
AUSTRALIA

Kiri Martin
Transworld Publishers (NZ) Ltd
Cnr. Moselle and Waipareira
Avenues
Henderson
Auckland
NEW ZEALAND

All Bantam and Young Adult books are available at your bookshop or newsagent, or can be ordered from the following address: Corgi/Bantam Books, Cash Sales Department, PO Box 11, Falmouth, Cornwall, TR10 9EN.

Please list the title(s) you would like, and send together with a cheque or postal order to cover the cost of the book(s) plus postage and packing charges of £1.00 for one book, £1.50 for two books, and an additional 30p for each subsequent book ordered to a maximum of £3.00 for seven or more books.

(The above applies only to readers in the UK, and BFPO)

Overseas customers (including Eire), please allow £2.00 for postage and packing for the first book, an additional £1.00 for a second book, and 50p for each subsequent title ordered.

THE SADDLE CLUB

Bonnie Bryant

Share the thrills and spills of three girls drawn together by their special love of horses in this adventurous series.